DANCER IN DARKNESS

A HALLEY BROWN MYSTERY

LEAH R CUTTER

KNOTTED ROAD PRESS

Reviews
It's true. Reviews help me sell more books. If you've enjoyed this story, please consider leaving a review of it on your favorite site.

Come someplace new…
Are you a traveler? Do you enjoy exploring strange new worlds, new cultures, new people?

Journey into the various lands envisioned by Leah Cutter.

Sign up for my newsletter and I'll start you on your travels with a free copy of my book, *The Island Sampler*.

I will never spam you or use your email for nefarious purposes. You can also unsubscribe at any time.

http://www.LeahCutter.com/newsletter/

Mysteries

The Purloined Letter Opener

The Rabbit Mysteries

The Shredded Veil Mysteries

Forgotten Gods

A Wind Blown Torment

A Stone Strewn Clash

A Sea Washed Victory

Tanish Empire Trilogy

The Glass Magician

The Desert Heart

The Ghost Dog

The Cassie Stories

Poisoned Pearls

Tainted Waters

Spoiled Harvest

Bloodied Ice

The Witch's Progress

Circle of Air

Circle of Water

Circle of Fire

Circle of Earth

Seattle Trolls

The Changeling Troll

The Princess Troll

The Fairy-Bridge Troll

The Troll-Demon War

The Troll-Human War

The Troll-Troll War

The Shadow Wars Trilogy

The Raven and the Dancing Tiger

The Guardian Hound

War Among the Crocodiles

The Chronicles of Franklin

Franklin Versus The Popcorn Thief

Franklin Versus The Soul Thief

Franklin Versus The Child Thief

Huli Intergalactic - Science/Space Fantasy

Origins

The Strawberry Girl

Contemporary Fantasy

Siren's Call

The Immortals' War

DANCER GLORIED in their latest art installation. It was mesmerizing, how the body floated high above the stage, how the boy's mangled legs had the appearance of movement even though the hunks of meat were still, how the streaks of blood gave color and the appearance of life to their creation.

It looked flawless from all angle, though Dancer's favorite view was from the back, of course. Dancer had spent hours perfecting the web of knots that tied the boy's arms behind him, a masterpiece of *kinbaku*. They had extended their artful knots to the noose around the boy's neck that hung him from the rafters above the stage.

The legs had presented a challenge. Dancer had put the boy's torn, bloody pants back on the body, and then used two bars with padded cuffs to separate them, a shorter one for the thighs and a longer one for the ankles. Dancer knew better than to hope that the audience would interpret their representation of frenzied dance correctly.

Dancer grew excited watching their creation sway above the stage. Though that awkward bit of flesh between their legs had been removed ages ago, all the feelings still seemed to center there. Dancer took photos on the phone they'd bought specifically for this purpose. It had never connected to a cell phone tower—it was only used as a camera. Later, they would pore over the photographs, relive every bit of perfection, pleasure themselves again and again. Maybe even get out the big blue dildo, ride it to ecstasy.

This stage was the biggest yet that Dancer had used. The Gemini Ballroom—an old dance hall that still held dances. The wooden floor had the perfect amount of give for dancing, and high metal beams for mounting stage lights. Dancer had spent weeks slowly accumulating their supplies backstage so that everything was set for the night of their big creation.

Dancer had created their first art installation in a tiny black box theatre just north of Capitol Hill, Seattle. For the second one, they'd moved up to an actual stage closer to the heart of the neighborhood, and now here. They'd yet to choose their next location. Should they use the Egyptian, the old movie theatre just down the street? One of the performance halls on the community college campus? Or would they move out of the Capitol Hill neighborhood and up to the U District, to one of the larger venues there?

Decisions, decisions.

Dancer would spend the next six months scouting locations and planning every detail, fantasizing about the next art installation, positioning the body, coming up with the perfect phrase. These were the high point of their genius, the meticulous crafting of the entire experience.

The kill was almost secondary, though still exciting. They probably would have to kill another submissive in between times, before the next big show. It would have to be another faceless victim, one no one would miss.

Those deaths were just practice. Every artist needed to practice their art. However, those bodies would be burned or buried—not displayed for all to see and marvel at.

Dancer had left their calling card as usual. They had titled this piece *A Lynchable Lindy-Hop*. Blood dripping from the body had already artfully splattered the paper. Next time, Dancer would have to give more thought to the pattern of the droplets. They'd stuck long knitting needles through the boy's cheeks, through his nipples, the fleshy parts of his legs, his penis, and elsewhere.

They grew more excited remembering the boy's howls when Dancer had first pierced his nipples with a specially sharpened darning needle. He'd already been tied by then, had fallen under Dancer's spell and cooperated.

They all did. They all wanted to submit, to be a part of Dancer's perfection. They just needed a firm hand. Most of them longed for the kiss of the flogger, the sting of the whip. They needed to only be shown once how to bend and pray at Dancer's feet. Gladly they gave up their agency to Dancer, their true and proper master, who controlled not only how they lived but how they died.

Another drop of blood spattered the stage, near the boy's driver's license that Dancer always thoughtfully left behind.

The boy had been a waste, his life quickly going down the drain. The least he could do was to die well for Dancer's art, to become something much bigger than himself.

Dancer knew that they had to be going. It was almost four AM. Corporate drones would start heading to their offices soon. Construction workers would begin to pour into the city from the suburbs, building more boxes for yuppies who would push honest laborers further out into the smaller towns surrounding Seattle.

Just one more drip. Dancer saw it forming at the tip of the needle piercing the boy's side. The droplet gained size, weight.

Just a few more seconds before it fell to the stage…

CHAPTER 2

Splat.

Halley Brown looked down at her jeans with dismay.

Stupid old-fashioned gas pump.

Instead of shutting off when the tank was full, the pump had kept going. The gas had splashed out of the tank with force, and now Halley had a large streak of gasoline decorating the front of her jeans.

Damn it!

She was not about to spend the next three-plus hours driving back to Seattle while stinking of gasoline. It was too damned cold to drive with the windows down as well. Though it wasn't raining, it was still November in the mountains east of the city.

Why the hell had she let her older sister Caroline talk her into stopping in the middle of nowhere? It had added at least ninety minutes to her drive home, back to Seattle, from Spokane. She didn't even like butter horns that much. But Caroline had gone on and on about how great they were, and how they were only available at this tiny, family run bakery.

Maybe Halley had felt she owed it to her sister to go and try them. Particularly when it had become clear that this had been just one of Halley's usual visits and that she had no intention of packing up all her belongings and moving back to Spokane to help Caroline with their mother or with Caroline's boys.

So now she had two of the damned butter horns nestled at the top of the cooler resting on the passenger seat of her RAV. Caroline had always insisted on packing enough food for the apocalypse for every trip, as if the journey would take days, not hours, and would be through hostile wilderness instead of civilized freeways with handy convenience stores. Then again, she had two boys, and claimed that it wasn't possible to be over-prepared.

As Halley put the nozzle back into the slot on the pump, the black monster truck behind her revved its engine. A faded sticker of a Confederate flag was stuck to the bumper. Each of its front wheels were at least two feet across, and the truck itself jacked up off the frame.

Hell, you'd need a ladder to climb up into that thing.

Though Halley had parked close to the pump, the idiot driver behind her had evidentially decided that his truck was too wide to go around her car, that there wasn't enough room between him and the station.

The old impulse to be an asshole rose up in Halley. For a brief moment, she considered slowly, very slowly, getting out a clean pair of jeans from the suitcase sitting on the floor of the passenger side of the SUV, then walking into the gas station and changing. Idiot truck was just going to have to wait until she was damned good and ready.

Halley pushed down on the urge. She wasn't that person. Not anymore.

Instead, Halley gave a friendly wave to the asshole behind her, got into her petite SUV and drove it around the end of the building, parking between the station and the woods that probably ran sixty miles without a break. Mostly pine trees, the few maples and cottonwoods already bare. Nothing killed the blackberry bramble running under the trees, of course.

The monster truck roared off.

Halley didn't bother trying to write down the plate number. Her dyslexia would have gotten in the way and she'd end up transposing the numbers or the letters. Even if she took a picture, she'd still have to double and triple check before she entered the numbers into the system.

What she did have was an extraordinarily good memory for faces and settings. If she ever saw that truck again, she'd be able to identify it. Even as a kid, she'd never lost when playing one of those games that showed pictures on cards, then flipped them over and you had to match them.

Three years working as a cop had honed those skills. Now, five years later, working as a private investigator hadn't dulled that ability at all. It had also improved her people skills. Or at least that was what she told herself regularly.

She couldn't hide behind her badge anymore. Couldn't really take her rage out on people. Not like that, anyway.

As for the asshole and the truck—Halley would remember his face and his vehicle for a while. There wasn't anything she could do about the guy being such an shithead, however. Not unless she saw him later on the road.

Maybe she'd be able to drive by laughing if the asshole had been pulled over or needed assistance. But that was about all the petty revenge she could manage these days.

Halley dragged out a pair of clean enough jeans from her overnight bag. The bright purple University of Washington sweatshirt that she had on over her T-shirt hadn't been splattered by the gas. She left her wallet hidden inside the arm rest between the seats, and her phone on the charger. She was only going to be a minute, and the car would be locked. Plus, no one could see the phone, as all view of it was blocked by the cooler.

The air still had that crisp feel of autumn, over the smell of gasoline and the cheap, greasy food that the station sold. It was only a little past three in the afternoon. Plenty of time to make it through the pass and to Seattle. No snow was predicted yet, but as it was already November, it could show up at any time.

Halley made her way to the station as the last of the cars at the pumps drove away. Left over Halloween decorations still filled the front windows, though it was almost a week after the holiday. She was surprised that they hadn't hauled out the Christmas trees yet.

She automatically cased the entire store as she walked through, on her way to the bathrooms. Too many years of playing "what if" as a cop. Rows of junk food running side to side, mainly chemicals, fat, and salt. Refrigerated cases along the back wall, filled with bottles of cloying sports drinks, but one case held eggs, milk, cheese, and soggy sandwiches.

The only other person in the store was the young guy behind the counter. He was Caucasian, early twenties, five foot eight. He listened to something on his headphones, his brown greasy hair bobbing in time. He wore an orange and red smock, a corporate design, over a stained white T-shirt.

The black-and-white surveillance TV behind him was showing cartoons instead of the aisles of the store.

It wasn't Halley's job to lecture the guy about the proper use of his equipment. Besides, who robbed gas stations anymore? Most people paid at the pump. Even those who didn't rarely used cash. The drop in convenience store robberies hadn't occurred because criminals had suddenly stopped committing crimes. It had been because the risk was no longer worth the reward.

The door to the women's room was against the back wall on the far side of the refrigerated cases. The light came on automatically when Halley walked in. The room smelled like bleach and orange GoJo hand soap, the kind mechanics like her dad had used. To the right were two stalls, black painted metal. On the left were a couple of sinks cut into a single gray counter. The mirror behind them had been scratched and tagged to hell. Pieces of stickers clung to the edges of it.

Halley glanced at herself in the mirror before she stepped into the handicapped stall at the back of the bathroom. Six feet tall, pasty white girl. In her early thirties, though she could pass for ten years younger. Easy going smile that she could fake as needed. Hazel eyes and a broad forehead, supposedly a sign of intelligence. Curly hair that frizzed in any kind of humidity. Despite the stress in her life, her hair was still brown, no gray—that probably wouldn't show up until she was in her fifties, based on how her mother had aged. Still fit, with regular workouts at the gym and the dojo, though it was harder now than ever to find the time for them.

As usual, she saw no resemblance between herself and the rest of her family. No one ever believed that she and Caroline were related, let alone sisters: Halley was lean, tall, and dark, while Caroline was short, plump, and blonde. Mom had always assured Halley that she took after her side of the family, but Halley had never seen it. She just didn't *fit* with the rest of the clan, particularly not her ambition.

With a sigh she turned away. After she'd done her business in the handicapped stall, she untied her shoes, slipped out of them, then the jeans.

Ugh.

The gas had soaked through the cloth. She bunched up some toilet paper and wiped her skin off as best she could before she pulled on the cleaner pair of jeans.

As Halley was tying her second shoe, the lights in the women's room went out.

Goddamn it! The place was pitch black. At least Halley

remembered the layout of the bathroom. Sensor must be near the door.

She squatted down and grabbed her gas-covered jeans. Before she could leave the stall, she thought she heard the door to the bathroom open.

However, the light didn't come on.

Something warned Halley. The air had changed. Grown heated, perhaps.

She stood silently, waiting just inside the stall door.

No one came in. The door to the bathroom closed.

What the hell?

Halley shook her head. What was she thinking? That she was some sort of Sherlock Holmes? Spidey senses and all?

She opened the door to the stall. The light didn't come on. Took a couple of steps forward. Still no light. Waved her jeans in the air.

That finally triggered the sensor.

Still, Halley felt spooked. Maybe it had been that asshole in the monster truck. Maybe it was just her own paranoia. After Halley washed her hands, she silently poked her head out of the restroom and looked around the store.

No cars were at the pumps.

Two people in the store.

The cashier. Who was slowly raising his hands above his head.

And the guy in front of him, holding a gun.

Scenarios raced through Halley's head as she assessed the situation.

She didn't have her phone with her. Even if she could have called for help, no one could get here in time.

Had the cashier hit the emergency call button? Probably not. Even if it was working, how long would it take for officers to respond?

The guy with the gun was shorter than Halley's six feet.

Skinny. The T-shirt he wore had once been a khaki green but now had black stains on it. The collar was frayed, and the jeans were ratty.

Shit. The hand holding the gun was shaking.

Meth? Fear? Or a combination of both?

Halley didn't have a weapon. It was locked in the car.

Damn it.

If she were still a cop, her CO would tear strips from her hide for not following the book and standard procedures. For not calling and waiting for backup. The rules were there for a reason. They saved lives.

Except when they didn't.

There wasn't anything else Halley could do. She had to stop the damned robber from shooting the idiotic cashier.

Because that would be an even worse end to her already shitty day.

HALLEY SILENTLY WALKED toward the front of the store, keeping her head down below the rows of shelves. The asshole with the gun still hadn't noticed her.

At least Halley had one thing working for her: the surveillance monitor still showed a cartoon and not the rest of the store, or else the robber would have seen her coming.

As Halley drew closer, she got a better look at the perpetrator. White male. Mid-twenties. Five foot nine. The pock marks on his face, as well as the sunken cheeks, proclaimed him a meth user. He was sweating though the shop wasn't warm, and the hand holding the gun was still shaking.

"Look, I told you, I don't have any more cash!" the clerk was proclaiming loudly.

Good boy. He'd given the robber all that he had. The money wasn't worth his life.

Unfortunately, the robber wanted more.

"See here?" the cashier said. He kicked a metal container under the register with his foot, keeping his hands up above his head. "All the bills go in here. I don't have a key. You can try to blast the damned thing open, but it won't do you no good."

"I need the money," the robber whined. "All of it! Now!"

"I told you. I don't have any more." The cashier was holding it together, not panicking. At least for now.

Halley thought for another moment, then acted.

What the hell.

She strolled right up to the front of the store and dropped her smelly jeans on the counter. "I need something for these," she interrupted. She looked down her nose first at the cashier, then the robber.

Rich, clueless white girl.

"I can't have them stinking up the Mercedes," she added. "Give me a bag."

The robber turned his gun toward Halley. "Give me your wallet."

"Who the hell are you?" Halley asked, putting as much of a pampered princess attitude as she could into her tone.

"I'm—it doesn't matter who I am. Hand over the cash, asshole," the robber said.

"Or what?" Halley sneered. "You wouldn't dare shoot me. Don't you know who I am?"

"Like hell," the punk said. He was completely focused on Halley now. Both hands were wrapped around the gun. His irises were pin pricks. He stank of rotting teeth.

Halley hoped that the cashier would have the intelligence god gave a goose and duck down out of line of sight. But he seemed too fascinated with the stupid rich girl to get out of harm's way.

A car pulled up to the pumps. Halley let her peripheral vision take it in, never staring at it.

Stay in the car, she ordered the nameless people there.

Her luck was never that good.

While the driver got out and went straight to the pumps, his companion made a beeline for the door to the convenience store.

"Hand over your wallet. Now," the punk said. He stepped closer to Halley.

Just one step closer.

The chime for the door sounded as the woman walked in.

As the punk started to turn away, Halley stepped forward.

She shoved the hand holding the gun up toward the ceiling, wrapping the fingers of her left hand around the robber's bony wrist. With her right, Halley sucker punched the robber in the kidneys.

One. Two. Three.

The robber suddenly became dead weight in Halley's grip. She let the robber drop, keeping hold of the man's arm and ripping the gun from his hand.

"Call 911," Halley ordered the gaping clerk still standing behind the counter.

"Dude! That was awesome!" the clerk said.

Halley rolled her eyes. "Just call 911. Tell them the suspect is already in custody." She wasn't about to reel off the code—the cashier wouldn't remember it long enough to repeat it.

After putting the gun to the side, Halley rolled the robber onto his stomach and brought his hands around behind him, grabbing the wrists. "You got any zip ties? Duct tape? Anything?" Halley asked the cashier.

Silently, the cashier handed Halley some black zip ties. Halley connected them together, then around the robber's wrists.

"No chance that you have a working security camera around here, is there?" Halley asked the cashier as she stood up.

The guy shook his head. "Seriously awesome."

"You might want to actually install some security measures in the store," Halley said sternly.

Dumbass.

Now, Halley was stuck here until the cops arrived and she gave her statement. She'd be lucky to see Seattle before midnight, barely enough time to unpack her car.

And though she set her own hours as a private investigator, she'd already arranged an early meeting with one of her recent clients. She wasn't about to call and cancel. The client wouldn't pay her until she turned over the evidence, proving that yes, his spouse had been cheating on him.

There was going to be coffee in her future. Lots and lots of coffee. As well as a fawning salesclerk who was already trying to figure out how to ask her for her number.

***

HALLEY BARELY CONTROLLED her speed as she spun out of the Podunksville police department parking lot.

Goddamn them all to hell.

Though sometimes she might miss the comfort of routine, she had *not* missed the shakedowns, the interrogations that cops gave each other for the field report.

Absofuckinglutely did not miss the rampant sexism, her every move questioned. If it had been a man who'd apprehended the robber? She would have received a pat on the back and an "attaboy."

As a woman? She'd been in that fucking police interrogation room for damned near ten hours.

Assholes.

Though no one had said anything directly, she'd known what they'd all been thinking. That the reason she'd left the force after three years was that she couldn't make it as a cop. Wasn't tough enough. Or disciplined enough. Or whatever enough.

Fuckers didn't understand that there was no way she was going to get *stuck*. Not like her dad had been. Not like her sister was now. Or the rest of her so-called family. No way in hell. She'd had ambition. Plans. Dreams. Hadn't realized that her dyslexia was going to hold her back so much when she'd joined the force, hadn't really understood that, as an army runs on its stomach, a precinct runs on paperwork.

Had discovered, much to her dismay, that she would *never* be able to write the reports the way that her superiors wanted. Which meant that she was always going to be stuck at the lowest level of the force, no matter how good she was at everything else. She'd never be promoted. Never move up to detective.

Not until she took her fate into her own hands and made herself a private investigator.

Halley took a deep breath and tried to focus. Brought her SUV back down to a reasonable speed after she climbed back onto the highway. She was determined to make it to Seattle and grab some coffee before she met her first client later that morning.

But she was never, *never* going to be happy about working with law enforcement. And if she had anything to say about it, wasn't going to be consulting them for a hell of a long time.

CHAPTER 3

THE SOUND of the front door to the shared office space slamming shut echoed sharply, as Halley's first client stormed off.

That certainly hadn't gone well.

Halley sighed and picked up the cup of coffee sitting in front of her on the conference table. Bright lights shone down on the pale, reflective wood, making the table seem larger than it actually was. It gave the room a more sterile appearance, less like the converted front sitting room of a mansion and more like a modern office space. She'd deliberately added to that effect this morning by keeping the blinds over the windows closed, as well as having the coffee already ready, sitting on the sideboard behind her.

If Halley had liked this client, she could have invited him into the large, warm kitchen area in the back, made coffee there while chatting about this and that instead of diving straight into business. Would have opened the blinds to show the circular driveway out front as well as the side garden with the rose bushes and emerald green lawn. Could even have brought in pastries, though that wasn't something Halley generally indulged in.

But she'd had a feeling about this guy. Particularly given how insistent he'd been that his wife must be cheating on him.

When Halley had provided him with the photographic evidence of the betrayal, he hadn't believed her. Said the pictures must have been staged.

That happened more often than Halley had expected, when she'd first started working as a private investigator. Fortunately, she'd learned to get the client's credit card number before she started her work, so she could just charge them if necessary.

If the client disputed the charge, she was more than happy to provide the credit card company with the results of her work. Normally, Halley would never share client information. However, as the client would be considered in breach of contract, she could give whatever evidence she had gathered to anyone.

That tactic generally shut the client up and freed her payment.

She took a sip of the sweet nectar of life and checked her phone. Next client was due to arrive in ten minutes. They'd booked using her online calendar. Halley was always happy to talk to anyone for thirty minutes for free. After that, it would cost them.

Having an online appointment system was a good way to get clients in the door. The free consulting let her screen them, to see if they had a case that she actually wanted to pursue.

She stood and stretched, yawning. It had been a seriously long night. She was still pissed off at the cops who'd questioned her until three AM. She took a deep breath, then widened her stance, letting her arms rise and fall, the first movement of her school of Tai Chi.

While she still regularly practiced Krav Maga, the Tai Chi centered and calmed her more.

The sound of the front door opening made Halley stop before she really got started into her form. The door to the conference room was still open, so she could see who had just come in.

That was *not* one of other people who rented the shared office space in the old converted mansion, that was for certain.

He—she—they, wore a beautiful purple evening gown that was tight against all their curves, showing off their impressive breasts. In addition, they wore a white fur stole across their shoulders, as well as a matching fur hat and white gloves. They looked like they were going to the opera, not to a meeting. They stood taller than Halley, maybe six four, though that might be the heels they wore.

They also had a broad, flat face with bushy eyebrows and sported a full, luxurious black beard.

"Ms. Brown?" the person said, spotting her in the conference room.

"Yes," Halley said, coming quickly around the table and making her way out to the entranceway. "Ms.—Mr.—Phoenix?" she said as she strode forward, her hand out.

"Just Phoenix," they replied, lifting both hands with the fingers widespread, then slowing circling them, indicating that they didn't shake hands. "So pleased to meet you, Ms. Brown." Their voice had a rich tone to it, somewhere between a tenor and a baritone. It was probably a marvelous singing voice.

"Call me Halley," she instructed. "Won't you come in? Can I get you some coffee? Or tea?"

Phoenix sauntered into the small conference room, a waft of patchouli and lavender flowing out from behind them.

"Do you have any green tea? Something warming?"

Phoenix asked as they sat themselves down at the conference table, looking for all the world like a queen awaiting her audience.

"I think we do," Halley said. She brought the entire caddy full of various teabags over to the table, as well as a cup and a carafe of hot water.

While Phoenix made their selection, Halley opened the shades, knowing that someone like Phoenix needed the extra light. Plus, she rather enjoyed the view of the winter garden, as well as the few maple trees that still held onto their splendid leaves.

After Halley splashed a little more coffee into her cup, she sat down across the table from Phoenix.

"What brings you in to see me today?" Halley said, sipping her coffee. She wasn't about to take notes, not until she was actually hired to do something. Plus, she hated trying to scribble anything down in front of a client. She couldn't spell worth a damn, and sometimes had difficulty figuring out what it was that she'd just written.

"Have you heard of Dancer in Darkness?" Phoenix asked.

Halley blinked, surprised. Given the dramatic nature of her client, she'd assumed that there would be a long, involved story of a cheating spouse and how they were doing Phoenix wrong.

"I have," Halley said, slowly putting her coffee down. Dear lord, she hoped that she wasn't about to hear a confession. But she hadn't read Phoenix that badly, had she?

"And their latest victim?" Phoenix pressed.

Halley thought back for a moment. "A drag queen named La Tonita?" She honestly couldn't remember more than that, what the victim's other name was. He'd been found the week before, hanging in one of the buildings nearby, a dance hall, in a gruesome display that wasn't appropriate for TV, despite the breathless speculation by reporters.

"Yes," Phoenix said. They looked as though they'd just tasted something sour. "La Tonita, or José, as he was known out of drag, was into BDSM."

"Okay," Halley said slowly. She seemed to recall that the victim had been tied up in an artful manner, appropriate to those who practiced such things. Come to think of it, all of Dancer's victims had been tied up in a similar manner, hadn't they? That had been one of the bits of information that the police had released.

Halley was certain that there was a lot that they weren't announcing though.

"The police are looking in the wrong place!" Phoenix announced dramatically.

"What do you mean?" Halley asked. Maybe Phoenix did know something about the case that the police didn't.

"José had a boyfriend. Someone he wasn't comfortable bringing to his shows," Phoenix said. "Everyone speculated about whether the boyfriend was real or not. But José had the scars to prove it."

"I'm sure the police are investigating every possible avenue," Halley said. Dear lord, she sounded like a spokesperson for the Seattle Police Department. Or worse, like the PIO, their public information officer, who dealt with the press.

"I'm quite sure they aren't," Phoenix said firmly. "They haven't come and talked to me, for one thing. I know everything that goes on in the community."

Halley doubted that. The community wasn't just a single entity. It was called LGBTQ for a reason, trying to give a lot of disparate factions a single face. No one would know about all the aspects of the various scenes that went on in Seattle.

Still, Halley didn't confront Phoenix about their claim. Instead, she asked, "Are you related to José? Listed as a known confidant or friend?"

"Details," Phoenix said with a wave of their beautifully manicured hand. "The police are too focused on the BDSM aspects of the case. Believe me, those people won't talk to the cops. And what Dancer did is so far outside of the bounds of proper behavior. The community is pissed off, and want to clear their name. The police need to be looking into this boyfriend instead."

"What exactly did you expect me to do about it?" Halley said, not wanting to waste any more of her time. "It's an active investigation. Even if I went to talk to the cops, they won't talk to me."

Not that she was still bitter about her last encounter with law enforcement. No, not at all.

Phoenix stared hard at her. "Not even if you have pertinent information?"

Halley sighed. "You should report that yourself."

"I tried," Phoenix said with an exaggerated sigh. "Walked right into the East Precinct police department. They wouldn't give me the time of day."

Halley grimaced. How much of Phoenix's story was true? The cops in the local precinct were actually really in tune with the locals who made up the colorful neighborhood. She'd been working out of the downtown precinct but had wanted to transfer to the one on Capitol Hill if she'd ever had the chance.

"What information do you have?" Halley said. May as well ask and see if Phoenix might know something that was useful, that the police could use.

"All of Dancer's victims to date have been homeless," Phoenix said.

Halley just nodded. She was going to have to take Phoenix's word on that.

"José was as well," Phoenix announced dramatically. "The police seem to think that he was still at his old apartment, out in West Seattle. But José was living out of his car. And the police aren't looking into that at all."

That could be important. Might not be. The police would discover the truth of the victim's apartment sooner or later, right? "Why does it matter that he was living in his car?" Halley asked.

"Because the cops need to be searching for it," Phoenix said. "He was probably taken from there. He was last seen performing at the Double-D, up on Broadway."

"But if it was the boyfriend, wouldn't José have gone along willingly? There wouldn't be much to find at the car," Halley pointed out.

Phoenix sighed. "There's still going to be evidence in the car," they said firmly.

"Are you certain that the police aren't already looking for the car?" Halley said. Because that didn't sound right. They'd be looking for everything related to José's life.

"They aren't," Phoenix said. "No description has been issued to parking enforcement. While I can't divulge my source, I have it on good authority that as of this morning, the cops are still not looking for José's car."

"Can you give me a description of the car?" Halley said, finally pulling out her phone and willing to take notes.

If Phoenix actually had some information that law enforcement needed, Halley would be willing to work as their go-between.

Besides, Halley knew Dick, the Detective in charge of the investigation. The only person on the force who she'd be willing to talk with at this point.

Her old mentor.

CHAPTER 4

Halley took it as a win that Dick was willing to meet her later that afternoon at Gaybucks, the large Starbucks on Olive Street that was only a few blocks from her condo. Though Halley was tempted to go take a quick catnap, she knew from experience that she was much better off pushing through the rest of the day and just going to bed early that night.

After Phoenix left, Halley cleaned up the conference room, carrying the carafes back to the kitchen and emptying them out, cleaning out both of the cups in the big farmhouse style sink, leaving them on the drying rack.

The converted kitchen was large enough that a catering crew could work back there for any office party that someone might decide to hold. It was the most modern room in the entire building, and held a massive gourmet stove, a huge butcherblock island with half a dozen stools around it, and a stainless steel refrigerator and freezer that had all the conveniences one could ask for from such a humble appliance.

Off the back of the kitchen was another sitting area that looked out over the back garden, an open porch that had been screened in and functioned as a three-season room, with a separate heating unit and huge signs reminding people to turn it off when they left.

Luther—one of the other people who rented space in the offices—sat out there on the end of the picnic table. He looked up from his phone and waved when she turned around, indicating that he'd like some company.

Halley considered another cup of coffee, but knew that her stomach would protest if she didn't eat something first. She picked up one of the satsuma oranges from the bowl on the countertop and went out to join him.

Luther was in his late fifties and looked it, his skin and hair both sagging and graying. He had at least two ex-wives that Halley knew about, as well as kids from both marriages. He did freelance medical dictation. Halley hadn't even realized that was a thing before she'd rented an office here three years before.

"Quite some clients this morning," Luther said.

Halley just shrugged. She never gossiped about her clients. She always considered whatever people came to see her about to be confidential, whether or not they'd signed contracts with her. She dug at the skin of the orange with her fingernails, the peel loosening grudgingly. The smell of fresh orange filled the small space.

"Got any more this morning?" Luther asked after Halley had peeled the orange, then managed to squirt juice all over the table when she separated the sections.

"Nope," Halley said as she mopped up the mess with a paper towel. "May go and do some surveillance." She had a client, Bridget Farrow, who insisted that her high-powered lawyer husband was cheating on her. Halley had been trying to dig up dirt on the man for over a month and had come back empty handed. Mrs. Farrow had insisted that Halley keep digging.

Privately, Halley was of the opinion that Mrs. Farrow was barking up the wrong tree. The man appeared to be faithful. Unless he was screwing his secretary on the floor of his office between meetings, he didn't have any opportunity to be fooling around. He worked all the time.

She'd even gone so far as to personally interview the man, supposedly to see if she wanted to hire him as a divorce lawyer. It had happened right around the time Chester, her ex-boyfriend, had dumped her, so some of the acting had touched real emotions, particularly when she'd talked about how he'd done her wrong.

However, Mr. Farrow behaved in the utmost professional manner. And his secretary had as well. There was nothing going on between them as far as Halley could tell.

She'd tried to fire Mrs. Farrow as a client, but had reluctantly agreed to follow Mr. Farrow around for one additional month, just to make certain.

She had time to go and see what he was doing for lunch before she met with Dick that afternoon.

"What fascinating new medical procedure have you been investigating?" Halley asked Luther. He considered it part of his job to stay on top of the latest medical tech.

He launched into an explanation of tiny brain sensors doctors implanted that would dissolve after a while, so the patient would only have to be operated on once.

As Halley listened, she found herself automatically reaching for her phone. She actually grabbed her own wrist to stop herself from checking to see if Chester had texted her.

They'd been together for five years. Halley was having to unravel a lot of habits that she'd built up over that time. Next week would be her one-month anniversary of being single again.

Halley's phone binged just as she'd started contemplating more coffee. Her adrenaline surged. Was that Chester?

Nope. It was Taylor, her best friend, checking in, making sure they were still doing dinner that night.

Luther, as usual, didn't appear to notice that Halley had tuned him out in order to text her friend back. Taylor had made it her mission to check in on Halley regularly since the breakup, making sure that she was okay. Before Halley had left, Taylor had insisted that they have dinner that Monday, as Halley was coming back from visiting family and was likely to need a shoulder to cry on.

Or more likely, a safe place to vent.

Halley let Taylor know that yes, they were still on, but it would be an early night for her as she hadn't slept all night.

It didn't surprise her when her phone rang two seconds later.

"Sorry, I have to take this," Halley said, slipping out of the back room. "Hey there," she said to Taylor. Halley walked through the house back to the front conference room, where she could talk without being disturbed or disturbing anyone else.

"What the hell happened that you were awake all night?" Taylor demanded.

"I could have just decided to pull an all-nighter," Halley said defensively.

Taylor's snort of derision came through loud and clear. "Yeah, right. You cherish your sleeping time. Voluntarily giving it up is about the same as you deciding to give up coffee for Lent."

"Point," Halley said.

"So what happened?" Taylor asked.

Halley gave her friend an abbreviated account of the previous afternoon, the punk at the grocery store, then being questioned by the police for hours.

"We can cancel if you need to," Taylor assured Halley when she finished.

"Naw, going out for drinks and food would be good," Halley said. "Get me out of my funk."

"Sounds good," Taylor said. They agreed to meet at one of their favorite Indian restaurants that evening.

Halley checked the time. She still had an hour before she would need to get downtown to follow Mr. Farrow around.

Instead of indulging herself in more coffee, Halley walked up to the grand staircase up to the second floor of the mansion. Many smaller offices with closed doors lined one side of the upstairs hallway. The other was a large space with desks, cubicles, workspaces and computers that everyone shared.

Might as well spend some time learning what she could about the Dancer in Darkness case. She had a feeling that she was going to need it.

CHAPTER 5

THE PACIFIC NORTHWEST had its share of serial killers. Most of them stayed out in the woods. Few made the papers or as big of a splash as the one who labeled themselves "Dancer in Darkness" just had.

This was their third kill, or at any rate, the third one that the police had connected to the individual. The first two had been spaced a year apart, so it hadn't been obvious to anyone that they were dealing with a serial killer.

This, their third, was only six months after their second. In classical parlance, that meant they were escalating.

Chances were, they had already found or were even grooming their next victim, planning out their next kill.

Dancer always left the bodies tied up in a complicated set of *kinbaku* knots, a Japanese form of bondage. They'd all borne marks of sexual abuse. Dancer left the driver's license with the body, as if they wanted to help the police along. The kills were always put on a stage. The first had been found in a tiny black-box theatre, the second, one of the local play houses.

Phoenix had been right—the first two victims had been homeless guys. Or at least that was what the police assumed.

The first body actually hadn't been identified, as the ID left with it was fake.

The reports all listed Dancer as a man, which Halley just shook her head at. Sure, chances were that it was a white male in his thirties, a loner. However, didn't they get it? Chances were, Dancer, like Phoenix, was going to be androgynous. Or gender fluid. Or even playing at gender fuck. Who knew.

But labeling them as male in the reports was just asking for trouble. It meant looking the wrong direction.

La Tonita, the latest victim, played an over-the-top vixen at the local drag shows. Her character was generally the "villain" in any skit. She stepped on other people's lines, was always hamming it up, trying to steal whatever scene she was in.

José, on the other hand, was portrayed as relatively mousy and quiet. He was a Hispanic man, short, slightly pudgy, based on the photos that Halley found, balding on top with just a little bit of still black hair along the edges.

Halley studied the side-by-side photos of the drag queen and the man. The transformation was quite astonishing. She never would have thought that one became the other regularly.

Though maybe that was the point. Had the two homeless victims been gay? The news speculated that they were, though none of the official reports that Halley found said anything of the sort.

Of course, that meant the case was going to come under the scrutiny of a lot of the LGBTQ community, many of whom, like Phoenix, would insist that the cops weren't doing enough.

It was a tough place for law enforcement to be in. Halley didn't envy Dick. He'd have to be reporting regularly both to his CO as well as the PIO. The articles didn't say who Dick was working with, but chances were, it was going to be an "all hands on deck" sort of situation at the precinct, particularly given the publicity the case was drawing.

Halley finished up her research and left the office, walking back outside into the fall sunshine. It had rained every day the previous week. She was glad for the break in the weather, even if the wind blowing the colorful leaves along the sidewalk was chilling. The sky shone a pale blue, as if the recent rain had washed all the color out. People were out walking their dogs, of course, and though it was midday, more than one pack of students took up the entire sidewalk.

After debating for a moment, Halley walked to the bus stop instead of going to get her car. Luckily a bus arrived just a couple of minutes later.

While driving might have been slightly faster, finding a place to park would squander any time savings that she'd accumulated. Plus the fees for parking downtown were ridiculous.

Halley sat in a window seat, just behind the rear door, always her favorite location. She had clear lines of sight and could easily watch both in front of her as well as behind her. That was part of the cop training that she'd never get rid of, her situational awareness.

Chester had hated riding the bus with her. He'd grown up in the sticks, just outside of Rochester, Minnesota, and had never developed a taste for public transportation.

Sometimes the bus could be an adventure, something her ex had never understood. He considered it a necessary evil to be tolerated, at best. Today, the bus was pretty quiet. Couple of moms sitting at the front, taking their kids on a play date. Older people on their way to doctor's appointments filled in another half dozen seats. No homeless, at least not yet.

Halley idly checked her phone for email, news, what have you. She wasn't about to go up to Facebook or put in headphones and listen to an audio book. That would have been stupid. She was out in public, and by herself, no backup. Couldn't afford to be distracted.

Instead, she watched the continual construction going on around her, marveling at the new buildings going up, keeping an eye on everyone who entered and left the bus.

Pioneer Square had been cleaned up considerably, even in the decade since Halley had moved to Seattle from Spokane. Not as many homeless kids taking up space. She didn't often see drug dealers anymore either. Instead, the square had office workers braving the cold winds and sitting outside, eating their lunches, which had been her plan as well. Pigeons gathered in large flocks, full of bravado, begging for scraps. The few trees around the edges of the square had already dropped their leaves, which city workers had obsessively blown away, keeping the area clean for the tourists.

Halley stopped by a sandwich shop that she'd started frequenting as part of the case. They also served rich calzones. While she could pretend to get a "healthy" one with spinach, she instead chose her favorite, filled with spicy meatballs and mozzarella cheese.

The piping hot calzone warmed Halley's hands as she made her way back to the square. She managed to snag the corner of a bench recently vacated by two women. A pair of businessmen glared at her—they'd obviously thought it was their space by right of the fact that they were dressed more nicely than she was.

Halley stared right back at them, the icy glare that few challenged, that said she was ready to take them on and win.

They walked away, disgusted. Halley just grinned and took the first gooey bite of her calzone, sucking in cold air when she realized just how hot it was.

She had plenty of time to slowly eat, savoring each bite, and finishing before her target made his appearance.

Mr. Farrow. Caucasian male, mid-forties, possibly early fifties. Five foot ten. Full head of brown hair. Eagle-nose. Weak chin. Expensive business suit, today's model being navy blue.

Halley waited until Mr. Farrow was half a block away before she reluctantly gave up her spot on the bench to follow him.

He went to the soup place just a few blocks away. It was only open for lunch, and primarily served homemade soups. For Halloween, they'd added dry ice to one of the pots that always sat behind the counter, bubbling away. Now that Thanksgiving was coming, they'd added a pumpkin soup to their regular roster.

Mr. Farrow was predictable in his routine, leaving the office almost every day for lunch around one PM, getting a quick bite to eat, then returning promptly. He'd spend the rest of the day in the office, meeting with clients and doing paperwork. Since he worked as a divorce attorney, he rarely had to go to court.

Why was Mrs. Farrow so insistent that he must be fooling around? The first time, Halley had been willing to believe Mrs. Farrow, given the hours that the man kept, as well as believing Mrs. Farrow's claims that she would call the office when he was supposed to be there and would be put off by his secretary. Plus, she didn't like the way Mr. Farrow referred to his secretary by her first name.

It was only when Halley had tried to fire Mrs. Farrow as a client that Halley had pressed her client for more information, trying to find out if Mrs. Farrow had any evidence of a dalliance. There weren't any receipts indicating anything damning. There had never been any makeup, telling hairs, or perfume on Mr. Farrow's suits. Halley had followed him around every day for a couple of weeks. He never went anywhere other than the office, out to lunch, to the gym, then back home.

There had to be something that Halley was missing. But what?

CHAPTER 6

HALLEY TOOK the bus back from downtown, up to the Gaybucks on the hill. Cars waited impatiently in the tiny parking lot attached to the building for someone to finally finish their drink and move. Inside was crowded, as always. At least they weren't playing Christmas music. Yet.

They had both registers going that afternoon, trying to take care of the rush and prevent a bad review. Halley joined the longer of the two lines on the presumption that it would move more quickly as the male, bearded, still-smiling barista hurriedly took orders.

Dick was already there, standing to one side, waiting for his drink to be served. He nodded and waved at Halley as she came in, then made his way to one of the cleared tables in the corner.

He looked the same as he always had. Halley studied him from the line. Dick was as tall as she was, in a worn brown suit, beige shirt, and navy blue tie. He looked more like a retired professor than a soon-to-be-retired cop. He had a long white face with a strong jaw and thin lips that were generally pressed together to contain whatever politically incorrect thing Dick had just thought up. His gray hair was full across the top of his head, and he kept his face carefully shaved.

Halley got a cup of the special Winter blend, though she knew it was a risk. Some years, it was sublime. Other years, it was so completely burnt it made blackened toast seem sweet in comparison.

No doctoring it for her. Straight, black, and bitter. Just like her heart, or at least that was what Chester had teased her about more than once.

Asshole.

"How's it going?" Halley said as she sat down, taking that first sip.

Wow. That was fabulous. She was going to buy a couple pounds and stick them in the freezer.

"Crazy as only the holiday season can be," Dick said.

"Sorry to hear that," Halley said, nodding in sympathy. She remembered what the holidays had been like, how the expectation that everyone should be merry caused shortened fuses and more furor.

"Eh, it's all fodder for the book," Dick said.

"How is the writing going?" Halley asked, catching the clue.

Dick had been writing his police procedural detective novel for as long as she'd known him, so over eight years, and it had not yet seen the light of day. Possibly never would. He was always going on and on about the rewrites, complaining about balancing the details of the craft of policing with the need for an interesting story. Because no one really wanted to read about paperwork, but life on the force wasn't all about shootouts, either.

Halley listened to him grouse on for a while, nodding sympathetically. While she could read books, and retain the knowledge in them, it was still too much effort most of the time with her dyslexia. Audio books had been her gateway into the wonderful world of fiction, and she would treat herself with a new book when her scheduled allowed her to get to the gym regularly.

"But I'm sure you didn't come here to listen to an old fart complain," Dick said after a bit. "How is the private dick job treating you?"

Halley rolled her eyes. It was an old joke between them. Though Dick's full name was Richard, he insisted on being called Dick. "What is the worst that could happen?" he reasoned. "They're going to make fun of my name to my face? Instead of behind my back?"

So he always called her a private dick, while he was a public one.

"Had an interesting visitor this morning," Halley said. She wasn't about to claim Phoenix as a client, as there was no agreement between them and no money had changed hands. "They had information about Dancer in Darkness."

"Really?" Dick asked, surprised. "Why didn't he come down to the precinct?"

While Dick was good at sympathizing with suspects, getting them to believe that he was actually on their side, he was awful at picking up clues sometimes. Such as Halley not labeling Phoenix as a guy, but using a gender neutral pronoun.

"*They* claimed that they did, and that no one paid any attention to them," Halley said.

Dick sighed. "Do you know what it's like to be dealing with a bunch of drag queens who all want attention? Who are happy to complain to any camera they can find that the police aren't doing enough to find the killer of one of their own?"

"Yeah, I bet," Halley said. She still persisted. "But the person I talked with this morning did have good information."

Dick grew still for a moment, seeming to understand that Halley had something he needed. "Go on," he said. The friendly meeting had just turned serious, and Dick went from goofy, inappropriate writer to cop in a heartbeat.

This was where it was going to get tricky. Because Dick would be in his right to haul her ass down to the precinct for obstruction if she didn't tell him what she knew. There was no bargaining with him. But Halley tried anyway.

"What can you tell me about the case?" Halley asked.

"Nothing," Dick snapped. "You know that. You know better than to even ask that. There isn't anything I can or will tell you."

Halley nodded. She'd suspected as such. She also knew that Phoenix wouldn't like it.

Too bad.

Halley told Dick about how José had been living in his car, and they really needed to be looking for that, as chances were, he'd been taken from there.

Dick gave her a disgruntled look. "Wish you could have told us that, oh, say, yesterday. Before we wasted our time trekking out to his apartment in West Seattle."

"Sorry," Halley said. "Do you know anything about the vehicle José was currently driving?"

Dick peered at her through narrowed eyes. "Why don't you give me the model, make, and license number and I'll run it? See if you're anywhere close to right?"

That was certainly more cooperation than Halley had expected.

Then again, Dick was quite possibly lying to her, and wouldn't tell her a goddamned thing after she passed over the goods.

Halley gave him all the information about the model and make, as well as the license plate, holding out her phone so he could read it himself and she didn't accidentally transpose any of the numbers or letters.

Dick looked thoughtful for a moment. "You're saying this person came down to the precinct with this information, and was turned away?"

Halley nodded. "East Precinct," she added.

"Thanks," Dick said. "I'll look into it. Don't know if this matches what we have or not."

"That's it?" Halley said when he didn't say anything more. "That's all you'll give me?"

Dick shrugged. "You know the rules."

"It isn't as if I'm some noisy reporter who will go blabbing everything about the case to anyone who will listen," Halley said.

"What is your interest in the case, then?" Dick said. "You know we're under a hell of a lot of scrutiny from the press, as well as pressure from the upper levels. This thing is way too public. On top of all of that, I've been saddled with a new partner. Billy Evans."

Dick said the name as if Halley should have recognized it. "Oh?" was her only response, trying to draw Dick out.

"His father was police commissioner ten, twelve years ago. Shot himself," Dick said. "Seems Billy wants to follow in Daddy's footsteps."

"Is Billy a new transfer?" Halley asked. Might as well see if that was another possible angle.

"Lateral," Dick said. "Had been working out in Spokane after graduating from Gonzaga. Ten years as a cop, then three as a detective. Moved back to Seattle a few days ago as part of the transfer."

"How did you manage to get assigned to babysit?" Halley asked. "Did you piss off Renee again?"

Dick snorted at her. "Not sure I've ever known Renee not to be angry with me."

Renee Bellweather was the Sergeant Lieutenant in charge of homicide. She was going places, had a one, three, and five year plan and had probably already scheduled her captain's test. She was a tall African American woman in love with her curves, with a voice that belonged on a late night jazz program. She always wore bright lipstick and blouses that looked good on camera.

"No, I think Renee assigned me Billy because she doesn't care that much for him either. And you know the reputation I have at the precinct," Dick said casually.

Halley nodded. No one would call Dick a cop killer, not to his face. However, he went through partners pretty quickly. Despite that, she'd still gratefully accepted his offer of being a mentor.

It wasn't until later that she realized he was using her as a model for one of his characters in his unending novel.

"Maybe she hopes that you can train him up to be your replacement, old man," Halley teased. Dick was only two years from retirement with a full pension, and had been counting the days for a while so that he could turn his attention to writing full time.

Dick shrugged. "If he survives that long," he said darkly. He took a final gulp of his coffee and looked over at Halley. "Anything else you want to harangue me about? Or you going to let me go do my job?"

"Sure," Halley said, finishing her coffee and standing. It stung that Dick thought so little of her. But she should have known that no one in law enforcement would be willing to work with her.

You either had a badge, or didn't. The world had been so much more black and white when Halley had been on the force.

"If you get any other information about the case, let me know," Dick said.

Halley nodded, though she knew there was no way in hell that she was going to give Dick or anyone else on the force any additional information.

Before Dick could add anything, his phone sounded loudly, the shrill ringing sound of an old fashioned call.

Halley's own text message notification—a trilling electronic bell—went off at the same time.

Dick nodded at Halley and strode out of the coffee shop ahead of her. Halley stood where she was for a moment, checking her message.

It was from Phoenix. The message listed an intersection.

Seemed as though José's car had finally been found.

As Halley walked briskly back up the hill toward the Double-D, she heard sirens behind her.

Dick pulled out of the parking lot of the Gaybucks and rapidly made his way up the hill.

What were the chances that they'd received the exact same message? At the same time?

Halley didn't know who Phoenix's contact was on the force, but whoever it was appeared to be sending Phoenix good, timely information.

Not a fact that she was interested in passing on to Dick anytime soon.

The intersection that Phoenix had texted Halley was just a few blocks from the Double-D, west of the main drag, in one of the quieter neighborhoods. Old turn-of-the-century nineteenth buildings ruled the corners, while smaller, 1950s bungalows took up much of the rest of the street. Tall, modern townhouses had been sandwiched in between the smaller houses. Many of the older single-dwelling houses that had originally had a pretty garden as well as a garage had been torn down to make room for six or eight new residences: pretty much the fate of any house put up for sale in that neighborhood.

Both ends of the street had already been blocked off by police cars by the time Halley got there. Officers stood on the sidewalks on either side, not letting anyone pass. Dick's car was there, and he stood with some of the uniforms next to a tan sedan, which was the color of José's car. Halley assumed they were waiting for a search warrant to be issued before they started processing the car and the surrounding area.

It looked to Halley as though tickets were stuck to the front window of the vehicle. It had been parked there for a few days, much longer than it should have been, particularly if it didn't have a residential parking sticker.

However, it had taken a while for the plate to be run and for law enforcement to realize that they'd already found José's vehicle.

Halley stood with the other onlookers at the edge of the yellow tape, trying to get a glimpse of what was going on just a few feet away. Camera crews arrived just after she did. Maybe they were hoping for an interview and not just shots of the abandoned car.

"What a circus," came a disapproving voice from beside her.

Halley turned to find Phoenix standing there. They'd changed out of the purple evening gown and now wore a dress that was silvery and just as glitzy. Instead of the white fur stole, they had on a navy blue cloak, with a tiara sparkling on top of their dark hair.

"That's exactly what it is," Halley said. "Thank you for the information," she added quietly. "Seems you were right."

"Of course I was," Phoenix said. "Just call me Cassandra."

Halley smiled grimly and nodded. What else had Phoenix known about José before he'd died?

"So now what?" Phoenix asked as another police vehicle with its lights blaring and sirens going pulled up to the far end of the street, opposite where they stood.

"That's probably the search warrant," Halley explained. "They can't start anything without the paperwork already in place."

Phoenix nodded. "And you were never that good at paperwork, were you?"

Halley gave Phoenix a bitter smile. "Seems you know all about me." Whereas Halley knew nothing about Phoenix at all. Cassandra. Not even a last name.

She was going to have to correct that. And soon.

"You are better than they are," Phoenix said dismissively with an expressive wave of their hand. "Particularly since I am going to continue helping you."

"What are they going to find in the car?" Halley asked, since Phoenix appeared to know so much.

"Plenty of blood in the front seat. That was what alerted the poor traffic enforcement agent that something was off in the car," Phoenix said. "La Tonita's gowns in the trunk. Probably bondage gear as well, which will set all the cops into a tizzy."

"Is it just La Tonita's blood?" Halley said, keeping her voice low.

"No," Phoenix said. "José's." At Halley's look, Phoenix elaborated. "Drag queens don't bleed normal blood, honey. It's full of sparkles, sequins, and pain."

That made Halley snort.

"But there won't be any clues, or something as careless as a fingerprint, in the vehicle," Phoenix proclaimed. "Dancer's too careful for that."

"You sound as if you know them," Halley said.

"No, not know," Phoenix said. "Just suspect."

"Whoa, who do you suspect?" Halley said. She put her hand out to stop Phoenix from turning away but didn't touch them.

Phoenix still slipped their arm up and out, a classic self-defense move. They had a looked of shocked surprise, as if Halley had just slapped them.

That was interesting. Phoenix *really* didn't like being touched casually. Now that Halley thought about it, they hadn't shaken hands with Halley when they'd first met.

That spoke of deep trauma. Was Phoenix's name descriptive of their life? Of being someone else before a horrific incident, and how they'd risen from the ashes afterward?

Phoenix collected themselves, putting on a smile that even Halley could tell was fake.

"Please," Phoenix said. "Would you tell anyone if you just had a suspicion, and no actual facts? Would you want to ruin someone else's life that way if you weren't absolutely certain?"

Halley nodded and acquiesced. She understood that in a way that Phoenix, who was a civilian, actually would. A large part of the training of law enforcement was all around that exact question: making certain, without a sliver of doubt, that the suspect they had in custody had actually committed the crime.

"Besides, maybe you should ask Dick's partner, Billy Evans, about it," Phoenix added before they walked away.

Halley stood gaping in the middle of the road as more reporters swarmed forward, searching for that elusive shot that would tell them the entire story. Failing that, something gruesome enough to get them eyeballs.

How the hell was Dick's partner connected to the crime? For that matter, who was Phoenix?

Did Halley dare tell Dick about Phoenix? Have them brought in for questioning?

Halley was reluctant to bring anything else to the attention of the police. She knew that Dick could be abrasive, and she had no idea at all how Billy worked.

Plus, Phoenix had hit the nail on the head, the classic conundrum that law enforcement faced every day. How to pursue a hunch, a suspicion, without any evidence to back it up?

CHAPTER 8

When Halley realized that she'd get nothing more from the crime scene that contained José's car, she took her time walking back to the shared office space. She had dinner that night with Taylor to look forward to, and a couple of hours to kill in the meanwhile.

May as well put some of those investigative skills to use, looking up Phoenix.

The sky had stayed clear all day. As the afternoon drew to a close, the temperature had plummeted. With no clouds to hold the heat in, the air took on a distinctly crisp edge, and was likely to become fucking cold by morning. Leaves scurried around Halley's feet as she walked up the sidewalk. It would be dark soon. She was looking forward to Christmas as people would start decorating, filling the night with bright, colorfiul lights. Some had already gotten started, but not enough.

The shared office space was warm, making Halley realize just how chilled she'd gotten. She made herself a quick hot chocolate (using the heavy cream in the fridge to thicken the drink) before heading back upstairs to the shared space.

Luther was still there, pecking away rapidly on his

keyboard as he transcribed whatever records he listened to. He had a personal safe located at the far end of the room where he kept the tapes he worked with, and used his own laptop computer for the work.

While he could do his work from his apartment, he said that he didn't work well from home. He liked having an office to go into every day. It made him more productive, giving him a routine that he never varied from.

Halley preferred her own job. She wasn't stuck in the office all day. She got to go out on the street, follow people, improvise and adapt. She trained constantly as well, which included regularly going to both the dojo and the gun range. She had a concealed weapons permit, and though she didn't need training to maintain it, she did anyway, despite the expense of the ammunition.

Anna Marie was also there, wearing her usual 1950s housewife-inspired outfit, complete with her dyed black hair in a bob, bright red lipstick, and a blue gingham blouse. She worked as a computer programmer for a company located in San Francisco. Like Luther, she could work from home, and did most days. But she also enjoyed getting out into a shared office environment at least once or twice a week.

Halley nodded to both of them before going over to her own "office." The space she rented wasn't "hers." Instead, it was part of the communal space that any of the neighborhood digital nomads could use. Halley had considered renting one of the cubicles, but she didn't want to pay that much per month, particularly since she never knew, month to month, how often she'd be there. So instead, she paid a per-use charge, which most months worked out cheaper than a dedicated space.

The shared space had at one point been two smaller rooms, but during the reconstruction, had the wall knocked out between them. Gray temporary walls separated one desk from the next on the left side of the room, while the right was a series of long tables, all looking out the windows, with computers set up at comfortable intervals. A printer/scanner sat on a table at the far end of the room, shared by all. The internet was screaming fast in the office, much better than what she got in her condo. Plus, here she had a large screen, instead of her little laptop.

Halley wrapped her still cold hands around the mug of hot chocolate and sipped it while she tried a couple of different searches for Phoenix. It took her a while to find the performer's wiki page, given how ubiquitous the name was.

Turned out that Phoenix had been born Marc Tallent. No birth year listed. Had gone to Julliard as a singer and was classically trained in opera. That explained the amazing voice.

There were no dates listed in the wiki, but there was a note about how after taking a break from performing, Marc had returned to the stage as Phoenix, a gender-blending queer performer. For a few years, Phoenix regularly performed to many accolades. Then, perhaps three years ago, Phoenix retired again. Now, they taught singing and performance.

The wiki page wasn't that long, and didn't contain any pictures of Marc. Halley was pretty good at reading between the lines, though. Something had happened to Marc, something devastating, that had destroyed their life.

Halley didn't need to know what that something was. She just had to be careful, and step around those landmines. Always better to know they were there.

As she closed the wiki page, she found herself reaching for her phone again and had to stop herself. Damn it! She was not going to check and see if there was a message from Chester. Not again. She really needed to get out of that habit.

So instead, she looked up Billy Evans. He'd made a name for himself in Spokane by working in Vice. Then again, most of the cops in Spokane worked Vice at some point—the drug epidemic out there was really bad. Billy was credited with breaking up a drug and prostitute ring. Or at least that was what the PIO had claimed.

Police work was a team effort. It wasn't just Billy responsible for that bust. However, that the PIO acknowledged him could mean several things. He might have led the team. He might have been the low man on the totem pole and therefore the one assigned to reporting regularly to the PIO. Or possibly he had plans to be someone, like Renee Bellweather, and so had made sure that his name got mentioned.

Then Halley dug into Billy's backstory. Commissioner Evans had shot himself in his study, in his home. Billy had been attending college at Gonzaga at the time. There was speculation in the news reports that it couldn't have been a suicide, at least according to the family. However, the medical examiner's report stated conclusively that it must have been.

Bill had been a law student at Gonzaga, at least according to the old article. Had he changed degrees after the death of his father to criminal justice? So that he could get a job in law enforcement?

She found mentions of his mother as well. Matilda Evans. She still lived in their home on Mercer Island, had never moved away from the house where her husband had shot himself.

Matilda was quite wealthy, at least based on the number of charitable contributions that she was publicly thanked for, as well as the boards she sat on. Probably her money, as Commissioner Evans wouldn't have made enough to be able to afford a mansion on Mercer.

Since Billy had only recently transferred from Spokane to Seattle, was he living with his mother? Or was he living as far away from her as he could get, as Halley was from her own family?

And how was Billy involved with Dancer in Darkness? Had it been through one of his cases in Spokane? Should she tell Dick to look closer at his partner? Or would that be seen as sour grapes?

Halley had too many questions and right now, was honestly too tired to really think long and hard about anything.

Time to go laugh for a while with Taylor before collapsing into bed.

CHAPTER 9

As HALLEY and Taylor finished up the rice pudding dessert they'd shared, she heard the loud trill of a new text message coming in.

Halley jumped when her phone sounded. "I have no idea," she told Taylor as she brought out her phone. "Hopefully nothing bad." Couldn't be Caroline her sister, could it? Had Mom had another one of her alcohol-induced "episodes"?

The text was from Phoenix, announcing that they'd set up an interview for Halley the next afternoon, with Roxy D'Lish, La Tonita's "frenemy."

"That isn't from Chester, is it?" Taylor asked. The downturn of her wide, mobile mouth showed just how much Taylor disapproved.

"It isn't," Halley said, showing her the text. "Have an appointment set up for me."

She wasn't really sure what she was going to ask Roxy D'Lish about. What Roxy could tell her that she hadn't already told the police.

Still, Halley told Taylor a little about how Phoenix had

been in to see her, and was insisting that Halley follow the Dancer in Darkness case.

Taylor seemed thoughtful at the news. "Are you sure you want to get involved with that?" she said quietly. "As you said, the cops are already investigating it."

Halley nodded. "I know. I've told Phoenix that. I'm not sure why they think I'm going to be so much better at it than my old mentor, Dick." She didn't want to mention Phoenix's concerns about Dick's new partner.

Taylor snorted at that. "It's because you're better at most things than the local police."

Halley just rolled her eyes at her friend. Taylor was always solidly in her corner, no matter what. It was nice to have a friend like that. They'd met at the community college, during a women's self-defense class that Halley had taught, in part, to drum up more business for the Krav Maga studio Halley went to.

At first, Halley had wondered if Taylor was interested in her romantically, though Halley really wasn't into women. It turned out, though, that Taylor had just wanted to be friends. Taylor wasn't strictly bisexual, she called herself 70-30 on the spectrum.

"Why would it have been so bad if it had been Chester who'd been texting me?" Halley asked as she got back to the serious work of demolishing the last remains of rice pudding in the bowl between them.

Dinner had been divine. This place had the best butter chicken. And the rice was always fluffy and cooked with almond slivers. Halley hadn't realized that there was a difference in rice before she'd started frequenting the various restaurants on Capitol Hill. As simple as the dish was, they'd been to more than one Asian restaurant where the rice had tasted like soap.

Taylor rolled her eyes at Halley. "Do you really need to ask that about Chester?" She wore her usual fall outfit of flannel over a T-shirt, with a fleece vest. Generally none of the pieces matched. This evening's ensemble included a yellow and black shirt with a bright red vest, but Taylor made it work. She had straight mousy-brown hair streaked with gray from "living hard," at least according to her, though she had only just turned thirty. Her nose was almost an afterthought in her round head, particularly in comparison with her large gray eyes and the mouth that seemed to take up half her face.

"Chester wasn't that bad," Halley said, automatically coming to his defense.

When Taylor just looked at her, Halley finally sighed and relented. "Okay. Yes, he was that bad. And I'm better off without him."

"There you go!" Taylor said encouragingly. "He wasn't right for you. Too stodgy. You'll find the person who is. Don't stress about it."

Halley sighed. "I'm still just unraveling my life from where he'd been woven into it, you know? Can't even think about adding in someone new."

"I know," Taylor said. "But you can do it. You'll be fine."

Now, it was Halley's turn to roll her eyes at her friend. "You know, you kind of suck as a life coach. All you give is platitudes and no real advice."

"Much better as a drinking companion, I know," Taylor said grinning at her. "Too bad you can't go drinking tonight."

Halley shook her head. She was far too tired to even consider it. Even a small nightcap at one of their favorite bars up the street. She really needed to sleep, hard and long.

"Everything will look better in the morning," Taylor said, as if reading Halley's thoughts.

"Yes, Mom," Halley said.

"You haven't talked at all about what happened in Spokane," Taylor said after a few moments of scooping up rice pudding.

Halley nodded. "Yeah. It went as well as I thought it would. Mom's too dedicated of an alcoholic, you know? She's really good at hiding the booze. And Caroline wants to believe Mom every time she says she's quitting. That this time, she means it."

"I'm sorry," Taylor said.

"Yeah, me too," Halley said. "But it gives my sister the opportunity to be a martyr. Particularly since I won't come to my senses, now that Chester has left me, and just move back to Spokane to share Mom-duty."

Taylor's parents had had the courtesy of dying over the last few years, neither of them needing any sort of hospitalization, so she'd never had to face these things.

"You know that moving back to Spokane would be the worst thing you could do, right?" Taylor said.

"Are you sure?" Halley asked, just to see the horrified look on Taylor's face. "No, no, I get it. I'm staying here in the city where I belong."

"Good," Taylor said. "Now, I'm walking you back to your building and tucking you into bed so you can get some sleep and stop having these delusions of grandeur."

Halley merely laughed and agreed. They talked more about their families, their jobs, the sorts of things they were working on, whether Taylor wanted to accompany Halley on the next hike her group was taking.

Still, after Taylor had said goodnight at the street corner, not making good on her threat to tuck Halley in, Halley had to wonder as she walked back down the hill to her condo.

Did she have "delusions of grandeur," as Taylor called

them for even looking at the Dancer in Darkness case? Or was Phoenix right, and did Halley actually have what it took to get the case solved?

That night wasn't going to bring any answers, just hard frost and deep sleep.

CHAPTER 10

DANCER CHORTLED with glee listening to the news accounts. They had recordings from every major news channel, then flipped through them, listening.

Those fools were helpless. Hopeless. Dancer relished the sense of power they had over the witless talking heads.

The way the press had broken the story had been fascinating. First, there was an unknown altercation, which was why the police had gone to the Gemini Ballroom in the first place. Then, there were rumors of a death of some sort. Maybe there had been a shooting? A drug overdose by one of the homeless people who gathered in the park across the street? Perhaps even gang violence gone wrong?

Eventually, the police acknowledged that it had turned into a homicide investigation. It wasn't until a day later that they finally released the identity of the victim.

It made Dancer angry that the press immediately jumped on the news that the boy had been a drag queen. No one marveled at Dancer's art, how the body had been displayed. No one understood how beautiful the piece had been, how much of Dancer's true soul that they had poured into the installation.

The news accounts of Dancer's previous displays also had barely mentioned how the body had been displayed. Were the police thinking to punish Dancer by not reporting more about the condition of the body? Why did the police hide the beauty of the art Dancer had created?

Instead of commenting about the body, the art, the news casters speculated about hate crimes.

Then, those stupid drag queens got involved. Of course they would. They called the boy one of their own, though he'd only been on the fringes, at best. Attention whores, all of them. Desperate for any camera to be shone their way.

Dancer had devoted the entire day to watching all the various news programs over and over again. Listening to the fear in the voices of the newscasters. Even the drag queens seemed scared.

As well as angry.

Dancer laughed at their anger. Dancer was above such things. They had tamed their own raging beast, only letting it out to play occasionally.

As the evening wore on and no new developments were being released, Dancer had to rely on the recordings they'd made earlier for their entertainment, watching them in slow motion, seeing the police enter and leave the ballroom building. How carefully they'd brought the body out.

Was it still a living pincushion? Or had they removed the needles before they'd transported it? Dancer zoomed in on the picture of the body on the gurney, but they couldn't tell.

Then they spent time identifying the various police officers assigned to the case.

It wasn't until their third play-through that they paused the recording, zooming in more closely to get a better look at the first detectives entering the scene. The tall gray haired man in the cheap suit.

They knew that second figure, the one accompanying the tall man, though it took them a while to place him.

That was Billy. Billy Evans. Though they hadn't seen him in a long time, they still remembered him.

So Billy had come back to Seattle to play? And had been assigned to the case? How delightful!

Dancer had always planned on writing to the press as part of their grand plan. Maybe it was time to set that into motion.

The cops had all read the books on serial killers, trying to better understand them. However, Dancer, like the rest of their kind, knew that they'd been born this way. Yes, Dancer's home had been broken—abusive father, inappropriately sexually-active mother—those forces had just honed the desires already there, born in Dancer's heart long before their environment could shape it.

Dancer knew about fantasy, violent fantasy, acting out, ecstasy, control, more fantasies. They broke the pattern. They were above such things. They were unique, special. No other killer approached them in terms of art and skill.

Though some of the books described serial killers as evil, Dancer knew that they, personally, were not. No, they were just better developed, further along the path, than most. What they did came naturally to them. Therefore, they weren't deviant.

While Dancer hadn't planned on addressing their audience, breaking the fourth wall, until after the fourth art installation, Billy being a member of the local police force made them consider changing their plans.

Not because they were reactive. No. They were in control. Dominating every aspect of their art, crafting their image as carefully as any celebrity.

They paced the broad living room overlooking Lake

Washington as they considered their plan. Yes, announce their existence now. Lead the cops on a merry chase.

The news of the locals finally finding the boy's car just convinced Dancer that they really needed to take control of the show, now, before the cops messed it up even more.

Yes, they could change around the timeline. Switch around who they killed next. But stick to the number of found bodies to only six.

Then, they planned to disappear for good.

Not that Dancer would stop killing. No, they were too advanced for that. But rather, they would work on new techniques, begin practicing a new form of the art of killing. Find a new state in which to practice.

Just because they'd been born in Washington, home of the serial killer, didn't mean they had to stay there.

CHAPTER 11

HALLEY SLEPT in the next morning, despite the fact that around six AM the heat turned on and she was soon sweltering. She still managed to fall back asleep and not get her lazy ass out of bed until closer to nine. The furnace was still in full swing at that point, and she turned on the fans to help cool her condo down.

Her building was one of the old, turn-of-the-nineteenth-century apartments that still had the original radiator heating with a single huge furnace in the basement. She could never control the temperature. It was either like this and she was sweating, or it was freezing. There was very little time spent in between.

While the heating left much to be desired, the condo association had replaced all the water lines as well as the tank. This meant Halley not only always had steaming hot water but also more than adequate water pressure, even though she lived on the top floor in a corner unit.

The shower helped Halley wake all the way up. Coffee would still be in her future. A lot of coffee. Luckily, this was Seattle.

Halley's condo was tiny, and barely qualified as having

two rooms, one being the kitchen, and the other the living room/bedroom. Fortunately, the closet was huge, almost big enough to be counted as a third room. It was as deep as the bathroom, though not as wide. A built in dresser stood across the back of it, with long racks on either side for hanging clothes. She also kept her gun safe in there, tucked into the corner, with her Glock safely ensconced inside.

Most days, Halley didn't bother going armed. That had been the biggest adjustment for her, after she'd left law enforcement. She still maintained a higher situational awareness than most civilians, always assessing any possible threat in a restaurant, never sitting with her back to the door.

Chester had made fun of her for it. Taylor, on the other hand, always checked in with her to make sure that a situation was safe before proceeding.

Yup. Taylor was kind of right. Chester had been that bad.

After getting dressed in her closet (and she could just imagine what Phoenix might have to say about that) Halley made her bed, then pushed the Murphy bed in the living room back up into place. She always kept her place tidy. It had been another way to differentiate herself from her parents and her sister.

Many of the turn-of-the-nineteenth-century apartments on Capitol Hill had built-in Murphy beds in the living room. While the mechanism of Halley's bed was new, to say nothing of the mattress, the location of it was where the original had been, built into the wall that was against the hallway.

The front of the original Murphy bed had held a fake mantel and fireplace. A previous owner of the condo had replaced that with a table that folded down, which gave Halley more space to spread out documents and work.

Halley went through her Tai Chi form impatiently that morning, though she knew that the movement would help her be more alert throughout the day. So she made herself slow down, going through the longer version of the form, until her legs were threatening to start shaking.

Finally, Halley finished her form and walked into in her one-butt kitchen, as Chester had called it. But he'd been right, and Halley actually really liked the fact that everything was so close at hand. She didn't cook that often—mostly it was stir fry with the occasional baked chicken or ham. The stove was on the same wall as the fridge. To her right was the sink with built-in cupboards above and below, as well as a tiny pantry. Behind her was the small table that frequently doubled as her prep space, as what little counter space she had was taken up with the coffee altar and her dish drying rack.

First, it was time for that sweet morning elixir. She had an Aeropress for making her coffee—she didn't need a fancy machine, a hand-press espresso was good enough. Particularly since she enjoyed her coffee black and had no use for a milk frother.

Breakfast that morning was steel-cut oats that she'd set to soaking overnight, with berries and more heavy whipping cream, plus a touch of cinnamon and cloves, heated up in the microwave. Thus provisioned, Halley went into the living room to sit at her desk and look over her email, see what was up with her friends on Facebook and Instagram, then scan all the headlines, looking for what was being reported about Dancer.

Seemed the PIO had made a statement about finding José's car, trying to answer why it had taken the police so long to run the plate of the obviously abandoned car.

Halley grimaced in sympathy as she finished up her breakfast. She understood that this sort of thing happened, even in the tightest run investigations. It wasn't sloppy work, but rather, large databases that didn't talk to each other.

After the news had finished, Halley closed her laptop, then went and made herself a second cup of coffee . She found herself trying to establish a timeline for the killing. La Tonita had performed Saturday night. The body had been discovered Thursday morning. Police couldn't say exactly when José had been killed. Poor José had been tortured before being displayed and hung above the stage.

Had José been taken Saturday night, or rather, early Sunday morning? When had he been killed? Had Dancer had the body for a few days, playing with it? Arranging it?

Not many serial killers practiced kills that elaborate. Most were quite quiet about their kills. Dancer must have been a performer.

Was that the connection? Between Phoenix and the serial killer? Had Dancer come in for lessons at one point?

And what was Billy's connection? Was there one? Halley found herself believing Phoenix on that account. For all of Phoenix's dramatic flair, Halley didn't think that they'd make something up like that.

Where were the three connected? Did Halley really want to spend her time looking into them, when she had her own cases to solve?

Armed with her second cup, Halley went back out into her living room to start doing her own, actual job. The one she got paid for.

Kind of.

This morning, though, instead of following Mr. Farrow, Halley decided to drive out to Redmond, now that traffic had calmed down from the morning rush, to see if she could figure out what kept Mrs. Farrow busy all day long.

CHAPTER 12

HALLEY WASN'T certain about all the people who came and left the Farrow McMansion in old Redmond. However, more than one of them had been young men. Not handymen or even pool boys, but guys who looked like your run of the mill college students.

Was Mrs. Farrow tutoring all these guys? The couple didn't need the money, at least not as far as Halley could tell. The McMansion was new, two stories tall, taking up a huge amount of acreage. Three families could probably live there easily. Trees taller than the house filled the backyard, all bare at this point.

Surely, Mrs. Farrow wasn't projecting? Insisting that her husband must be having an affair when in fact, she was the one who was fooling around? It was an expensive mind game to be playing. Halley was making quite a bit of money off the case.

Of course, Halley wanted to believe the woman that she was being taken advantage of, that her husband was a hounddog. The stereotype existed for a reason. But she was starting to have her doubts about Mrs. Farrow, and the real reason why she was accusing her husband of being unfaithful.

Halley wasn't about to look up every single license plate that she photographed, but she picked a couple that were most likely, to see if she could find any information on the people visiting Mrs. Farrow.

However, the wife herself never made an appearance. She stayed in all through the afternoon, receiving visitors like a social maven.

Halley ate lunch in her car, a salad she'd gotten to go from her favorite little hole in the wall back on Capitol Hill, along with a couple energy bars. She'd found that she did better on stakeouts with small amounts of food regularly, primarily as a way to stave off the boredom.

Eventually, Halley drove off, needing the time to get back into the city before her interview with Roxy D'Lish.

Traffic was about as bad as Halley had thought it would be, and so she got back to the city and her car parked in its slot without much time to spare. She quickly walked back up the hill to the Double-D.

The entrance to the venue was directly in the center of the space. To the left was the bar, to the right was the performance hall.

The bar was open and serving happy hour. A couple of office drones were already there, seated at the high tables next to the brightly decorated windows, steadily drinking.

Halley hadn't been to the Double-D for quite some time. The venue had closed for a while as they'd undergone a much-needed facelift. The bar itself hadn't been changed much, not that she could tell from her quick glance.

Instead of seating herself at a table, she walked into the performance hall. It looked completely redone, with a new stage up front, probably new lights and a new sound system. The audience area was full of tables, now on three tiers, so that people at the back could actually see the stage. It was now large enough for close to eighty customers.

"Can I help you?" came a soft voice from behind Halley.

She turned and smiled at the waiter who'd come to collect his errant charge. He was Hispanic, with dark eyeliner and just a touch of pink on his lips. He wore the usual server outfit, black shirt and pants, with a black apron.

"I'm here to interview Roxy D'Lish," Halley said.

The waiter looked confused but said, "Uhm, sure. She's in dressing room four, getting ready for tonight's show. Do you want anything?"

"No, thanks," Halley said. The dressing rooms were back behind the bar. As a patron, she'd walked past them more than once on her way to the restroom.

However, this area had also been remodeled. The hallway to the bathrooms had been squeezed in. You could no longer walk past the doorways to the dressing rooms. Instead, Halley had to walk all the way to the end of the hall, admiring the brilliant sea mural that had been painted across it, then let herself in a door that explicitly stated, "NO ADMITTANCE."

The hallway containing the doors to the dressing rooms was shockingly bright after the darkness of the customer hallway. Bright yellow paint covered the walls and strong lights set into the ceiling burned down, making the cramped space warm. Framed photos of many of the performers covered the wall opposite the doorways.

There were four dressing rooms, all numbered, with sparkling rainbow stars painted on each. Halley knocked before opening the door to number four.

Roxy D'Lish sat at the far dressing room mirror. There was space for a second performer next to the door. Several costumes on movable racks took up most of the rest of the space.

"Hello, darling," came the smooth voice of the figure. "You're Halley Brown?"

"I am," Halley said, coming closer.

The person currently painting their face no longer looked human, but more like a caricature. A pale nylon cap held back their short dark hair. Their skin was all a single color—no contours had been added yet. Only one eye had been painted, with an over arching brown and brilliant, sparkling blue eyeshadow.

"Thank you for agreeing to meet me," Halley said. "What should I call you? Ms. D'Lish?"

The person snorted in laughter at that. "Do call me Roxy," she said. "I'm well on my way to becoming her, so would prefer that over my boy name."

"I'm sure the police have already talked with you about José, La Tonita," Halley started with.

"No, no they haven't," Roxy said, sounding very disgruntled. "I mean, we really were not the best of friends. You'd think the cops would want to find out about La Tonita's enemies. Though there were so many, maybe they just haven't narrowed down the pile enough yet."

"I see," Halley said. She hesitated. She didn't want to "poison the witness" as it were by talking to Roxy before the police had. Really didn't want some asshole attorney to claim that anything Roxy said was not relevant due to Halley's influence.

It was one of the reasons why the cops didn't want civilians involved in an investigation. Who knew what they might say? How the prosecution could use that against the case they'd built up?

"The only reason I'm talking to you is as a personal favor to Phoenix," Roxy said. "They're the only one who really appear to want this case solved."

"Why is that?" Halley asked. May as well try to get as much information as she could. "Was Phoenix heavily involved with La Tonita?"

Roxy laughed again. "Oh hell no. I doubt Phoenix even knew who La Tonita was before she was killed. Phoenix just fancies themselves as a grand communicator. They've got their fingers stuck in every pie you could imagine." Roxy turned again to the mirror and started painting their other eye. Halley couldn't help but watch, fascinated, as color, shape, and dramatic flair were applied.

"Phoenix claims that they know what is going on in every community," Halley said.

Roxy shook her head and rolled her eyes at that. "Yeah, sure. And I've got a magical strap-on to sell you if you actually believe that. You know, with the healing power of great dick."

Halley couldn't help but grin. She liked how irreverent Roxy was being. "But you still took Phoenix's call, and agreed to talk with me."

Roxy sighed and added a dark black stroke for her eyebrow. "Phoenix is trying to do the right thing with all that money of theirs. Now, don't you go repeating what I just said. Phoenix might make the mistake of thinking I have a heart and want me to start doing charity events if I'm not careful."

"No charity events. Got it," Halley said. Though she'd never suspected Phoenix of being rich. Then again, their outfits indicated a certain level of wealth. "According to Phoenix, you were La Tonita's greatest frenemy?"

"Yes, darling, I was," Roxy said. She faced the mirror but still caught Halley's eye in it. "Couldn't help it. José was a mousy boy. Utter sub. Just waiting for someone to order him around. While La Tonita was a bossy bitch. Didn't respect anyone else, didn't give anyone else the space for their art. Walked on other people's lines all the time, always upstaging whoever she was performing with."

"Why did anyone put up with that?" Halley asked.

"Because she was so damned good at it," Roxy admitted. She added more of the brilliant, sparking blue eyeshadow. "When drag queens insult each other, it's called throwing shade."

Halley nodded. She knew that, but she appreciated Roxy spelling it out.

"La Tonita was better at throwing shade than anyone else. She could read a person, figure out what was in their soul, then make fun of it for all the world to see. It's quite an art, to be able to read someone you've just met. And La Tonita was great at it."

"So she insulted everyone?"

"No, not just that. She made it funny. Everything that came out of her mouth would make you laugh, even as you felt angry and embarrassed."

"Do you think another drag queen killed La Tonita?" Halley had to ask.

Roxy paused long enough that Halley wondered if she'd crossed some invisible line by suggesting the possibility.

Finally, Roxy replied, "You know that José had a boyfriend, right?"

"I've been told that, yes," Halley said.

"La Tonita had a big, loud, obnoxious personality," Roxy said with the perfect dramatic sigh. She'd finished her eyes and moved on to painting her lips. Halley watched, mesmerized, as Roxy applied outliner, then three different shades of lipstick for the perfect blend.

"But José, José was a mouse. Quiet, subdued. You'd never imagine that he'd say, let alone even think, what La Tonita did," Roxy said. She turned to look directly at Halley. "While a few drag queens have that sort of split, most don't. I'm just as brass as Roxy as I am as Devin. It made José unpopular, though, particularly given how insulting La Tonita was. You'd look at that quiet boy in the corner and just imagine all the shit he was making up in his head about you, but was too good to say any of it."

"That made José, as well as La Tonita, very isolated, didn't it?" Halley said, trying to put the pieces together.

"Gold star, my dear!" Roxy said, turning back around to start contouring her face. "Which was particularly biting, given how much more closely the community has banded together in our current political climate. So it's understandable, really, why the poor dear might fall prey to a boyfriend who'd use him up."

"What do you mean?" Halley said. "Use him up how?"

Roxy gave a dramatic sigh. "José, bless his heart, was a sub. Very submissive."

Halley nodded, understanding that Roxy was talking about BDSM and not just a personality trait.

"He found himself a nasty master who was taking over every aspect of his life," Roxy said. "Always having to call and check in. Always touching the pretty little lock around his neck. It was his master's idea that José give up his apartment and start living in his car." Roxy sighed and shook her head. "Now, a little role play can be fun for everyone. But José was starting to be in the lifestyle twenty-four/seven."

"So you think this boyfriend killed José?" Halley asked.

"What is the ultimate submission but to give up your life?" Roxy replied. "The problem is that none of us ever met the boyfriend. Some of the girls thought the boyfriend didn't really exist. Who would want a mouse like José? But I knew." Roxy turned again, her face dramatically beautiful with high cheekbones now, a narrow chin, and a dramatic flare of blue eyeshadow over each eye. "I knew he was real. Saw the scars on José's back from where he'd been beaten. Even the most dramatic of queens wouldn't do that to themselves."

Halley would give just about anything to be able to read

the medical examiner's report, to see if she could find evidence to back up Roxy's story.

Before she could ask another question, the door to the dressing room opened.

Dick came walking in, along with his new partner, Billy. Dick glared at Halley but didn't say anything to her. Instead, he addressed Roxy. "Devin Montgomery. I'm Detective Wilkerson, this is Detective Evans. We have a few questions for you."

"I've said all I'm going to say to her," Roxy said, pointing at Halley with a sharp eyebrow pencil. "Y'all can talk to my lawyer."

The temperature in the small dressing room rose about ten degrees as Dick started to fume.

"Mr. Montgomery—" he started.

Halley couldn't help but roll her eyes. Really, Dick needed to catch a clue. He was no longer talking to Devin, but to Roxy. And unless he started to address her properly, she wasn't about to say one word to him.

"I have a show to put on," Roxy interrupted. "And all of you need to leave my dressing room. Or I'm going to call my lawyer, then every queen I know, and you're going to have a public relations nightmare on your hands. I can guarantee it."

Halley didn't like the glint of mischief that came to the drag queen's eye. She was obviously dying for a confrontation.

"Dick," Halley said quietly, before he said something that everyone was going to regret.

He glared at her, but nodded after another moment. "We'll be in touch, Mr. Montgomery," he said, then he stomped out of the dressing room, Billy in tow.

Halley wasn't about to apologize for her mentor. He was just doing what he always did, being a cop first. How he'd managed to get this far without being able to read a room had always astounded her.

"Thank you for your time, Roxy," Halley said.

"It was worth it, darling, just to see the look on their faces," Roxy said with a devilish grin. "You ever want to come see a show, you just send me a note. I'll make sure you have VIP tickets, up front."

"Thanks," Halley said. She had no idea if she'd take her up on it. Then again, Taylor might think it was a fun night out.

However, even the promise of free tickets wasn't going to make up for the fight that Halley was about to have with her former mentor.

Halley paused for a moment, mentally pulling up her big-girl panties, before heading out to the bar to face the music.

CHAPTER 13

Halley made it all the way to the door leading out to the street before she saw Billy. He jerked his head to the side, indicating that Halley should follow him to the stage portion of the Double-D. It appeared that Dick had commandeered the space for her interrogation.

Halley considered it a win—at least he wasn't hauling her ass down to the precinct to question her, though she knew that was still a possibility.

Billy and Dick sat on one side of a long table at the far side of the room, a chair pulled out on the other side, obviously where they wanted her to sit.

With her back to the door, of course. Just one more thing to make her uncomfortable.

Halley still sat down, leaning back in the hard wooden chair, affecting an air of nonchalance.

A waiter followed her into the space, the young man she'd seen before, with the dark, Hispanic looks and the newly-applied bright pink lipstick. He flamboyantly placed napkins down in front of the three of them. "What can I get you?" he asked.

Halley noted the defiant tone in his voice. He'd already

identified the two men and decided to come in just to fuck with the police. She felt a little better, a little less intimidated, that someone else besides Roxy was on her side.

"Nothing," Dick said in a harsh tone. Billy just nodded.

Halley looked up and smiled at the boy. "I'll have a margarita," she said. "On the rocks."

The waiter smiled at her and gave her a broad wink before he sashayed out of the room.

Dick looked angry enough to spit nails. "Why did you do that?" he asked.

Halley maintained her calm instead of diving into guilt. "This is just a friendly conversation between colleagues," she said. "Not an inquiry into my behavior as a law enforcement official."

"We are not colleagues," Dick said firmly. "You are a civilian. Nothing more."

Halley swallowed and nodded. "Things aren't really that black and white," she maintained.

"No," Dick said. "You have information. You will give it to us. Or I'm hauling your ass down and throwing you into the general population at the jail. And you know how well they'll treat you, once they learn that you were once a cop."

Halley felt her smile grow brittle. She wasn't certain if it was an empty threat or not. Dick was angry enough, and mean enough, that he just might do that.

"And instead of calling a lawyer, I'm going to call Roxy and all the other drag queens. See how well that sort of decision is going to look in the bright light of news cameras," Halley replied, maintaining a casual tone despite how threatened she felt.

Dick sighed explosively and leaned back, as if trying to decide whether he should just shoot her now or wait until she was out on the street.

Billy leaned forward, trying to play peace maker. "We

know you want to catch this killer, just the same as we do. We're all working toward the same goal. Let's try to keep that in mind."

Halley turned to study Billy. It was the first time she'd seen him close up. He had classic American leading man good looks, with a cleft chin, broad forehead, and deep, penetrating eyes. His skin was as pale as any office worker's, and his hair was dark, curly, and frizzy like hers, or it would be, except he kept it cut close to his head. They were the same age, in their mid-thirties. They both had fathers who'd killed themselves, though in Halley's case, her father had worked himself to death rather than eating a gun.

In another life, they might have been friends.

Now, a gulf much wider than the table they sat at separated them.

"So, now that we're all on the same page," Billy said after a few moments, giving Dick a look, "tell us what you learned."

Halley couldn't help but roll her eyes. Billy may have tried to say it more politely, but the message was the same. Talk to us, or there will be *Consequences*.

The waiter came back before Halley could say anything more. He presented her with a huge margarita. The top of the glass was bigger than her head.

When Halley reached for her wallet, he assured her, "Oh, no, honey. It's on the house. For you." He added a glare at the cops for good measure. "My name is Roland. You want anything, you just ask."

After a second glare at the cops, Roland strolled out of the theatre area.

Halley just shook her head and tried to bite back her grin. Then she took a sip of her drink, just to fuck with the cops on the other side of the table.

Fortunately, it was really good. More sour than sweet,

and the kick of alcohol that flowed down her throat added warmth, rekindling the fire in her belly.

Bring it.

She relayed the conversation she'd had with Roxy to Billy and Dick, talking about the separate personalities of José and La Tonita, as well as how isolated they'd been from the community as a result.

Billy took notes while Dick asked questions, making sure that Halley told them everything, all her impressions as well as her information.

Finally, Halley was finished. She'd only taken a couple of sips of the margarita. She needed to stay level headed through all of this, though she could imagine chugging it when they were all finished.

"Why were you here in the first place?" Dick asked. "Why were you interviewing Devin?"

Halley shook her head at the denseness that her mentor was displaying. "I wasn't interviewing Devin. I was interviewing Roxy. She was halfway transformed by the time I showed up."

"You're kidding, right?" Dick said with a deep growl.

Halley gave Billy a glance, to see if he at least understood what she was trying to say.

Billy nodded. "It's important to them," he said quietly. "You have to know who you're talking with."

"Exactly," Halley said. She paused, then figured, what the hell. "It's basic police work one-oh-one. Build rapport with whoever you're interviewing. But also, you have to realize that your victim had a similar split in personalities."

If someone could bottle that glare of Dick's, they could possibly use it to fry eggs. At least Billy appeared to take the gentle reminder to heart.

"You still haven't answered the question," Dick said. "Why interview Roxy D'Lish?"

Halley was impressed that Dick at least appeared to take the hint. "Everyone knew that Roxy was La Tonita's greatest frenemy."

"No," Dick said after a few moments. "Everyone did not know that. It wasn't part of their schtick, when they were on stage. Where did you get your information about Roxy D'Lish?"

"I told you before. I had someone in the community come to me to express concern about the case, as well as how law enforcement was handling it," Halley said. "As they're a client, I cannot say more." She was stretching the truth, but she figured that Phoenix would back her up if asked.

Dick sat back in his chair, still considering whether or not it was worth the publicity to throw her in jail.

"They did have one other interesting conjecture that I wanted to share," Halley said after a few moments. She turned her attention on Billy. "My client does not know who Dancer is. However, they suggested that you might."

Billy looked stunned. "Me?" he said, his usual smooth voice cracking slightly.

Halley shrugged. "I don't know for certain. But my client's information has been solid before now. Food for thought."

"I suggest that you bring this client with you to the precinct," Dick said. "Say, ten AM tomorrow. So that we can all catch up on the latest."

"All I can do is ask," Halley said, though she had no intention of doing anything like that.

"No, you will explain to them that this time, they will be listened to," Dick insisted. "Or else I'll subpoena your records. What kind of a field day would the press have with all your client information?"

She could imagine how such a slip up might occur on the part of the police department, how sorry they would be that such a breach occurred, assuring the public that it would never occur again. Dick was possibly that angry right now to consider doing such a thing.

It would ruin her.

"You would never be able to convince a judge of probable cause," Halley said firmly. "I will see if I can bring my client down to headquarters tomorrow. But also? If we aren't treated well, and by that, I mean in a timely manner, we're both walking. You hear me?"

"Of course," Dick promised smoothly.

Halley snorted and shook her head. She almost felt sorry for him and what he was facing when he sat across the table from Phoenix.

CHAPTER 14

HALLEY AND PHOENIX sat together in the community meeting room of the downtown precinct. Halley had refused to be shunted off to a suspect interview room, so Dick had dropped them off here before he'd been called away.

The community room was much nicer than an interview room, with a large oval wooden table taking up much of the space, and chairs that wouldn't instantly rack up your back by sitting on them for any length of time. Flags stood at the front of the room. Hallcy had a vague memory of some of the press conferences being held here. Large TV monitors hung silently from the two front corners.

As it was a meeting room, windows lined the wall, giving a great view of everyone coming and going into the station.

Phoenix wore a dark red gown that morning, and long, matching opera gloves that went up to their elbows, so they had bare shoulders that showed a surprising amount of muscles. In addition to the usual tiara, Phoenix had on matching earrings that brushed their shoulders, as well as a gorgeous necklace that also sparkled.

In comparison, Halley felt positively dowdy in her usual attire, a Henley in a pretty turquoise over a pink T-shirt, jeans, and black ankle boots. Her leather jacket was slung over one arm of the chair. They both had brought their own coffee, and now sat and waited.

Dick had promised them a timely interview. Halley already had a timer on her phone set. She was only willing to wait a short while. She didn't know if Dick had been called away by something actually important, or if he'd made up something as a way of "sweating" them and making them wait.

A tall blond man walked past the windows, then paused.

"That's Warren Strauss," Phoenix said. "Owner of KULO news."

"Really?" Halley said. She remembered reading something about that this morning. She pulled out her phone and opened it to the news site. "They claim that the killer known as Dancer in Darkness has contacted them, promising them more details in exchange for an exclusive interview."

While Phoenix read the announcement on Halley's phone, Halley slid her chair to the end of the table so she could get a better look at Warren, who had paused. He wore a nice gray suit, white shirt, and red power tie. His dark hair was expertly trimmed. Wide, dark eyebrows set off his pale complexion, as well as his big blue eyes. He had a long, thin face with a huge beak of a nose. He looked pleased, as though he'd just found his prey.

A shorter man in a more expensive suit stood beside Warren. Probably his lawyer.

They had paused in order to talk with Renee Bellweather, Sergeant Lieutenant of homicide. She looked chic in a navy blue power suit.

Phoenix snuck over to the door of the conference room and opened it a crack, before coming over to sit beside Halley.

Halley was torn. They probably shouldn't be listening to this conversation. However, chances were, Phoenix's instincts would pay off and they'd need to know what was discussed between those two.

She would have to tell Dick about it later. Except that there he was, hurrying up the hallway, with Billy in tow.

Billy did a double take when he saw Warren.

Warren reacted in a similar fashion.

Huh. The two of them knew each other.

Halley glanced at Phoenix, who had slid their chair beside Halley's. "High school," they mouthed.

"So you're the Billy mentioned in the letter," Warren started off with.

"What letter?" Dick asked.

"Seems that Dancer isn't happy with the coverage being given his crimes," Renee said. "Wants the public to know more. So he contacted Warren here, sending him a note, promising more details if the station agrees to give him an exclusive." She took a moment to glare at Warren. "And Mr. Strauss was only too happy to cooperate."

Warren just shrugged. His lawyer gave her a belligerent look. "We did bring the letter here."

"After you announced its existence," Renee said.

"We didn't broadcast the contents of the letter, though we were within our right to do so," the lawyer said.

"The letter has been turned over to forensics," Renee said. She shoved what was probably a copy of it toward the detectives.

Halley was itching to read the contents of the letter. She knew better than to ask either Dick or Billy about it.

Still. Phoenix nodded at her, as if thinking the same thing.

Could Phoenix get a copy? Was their informant at the police station that good? And if they did send Phoenix and

Halley a copy, should Halley tell Dick and Billy about the leak? After the case was finished? How much trouble would she get in?

"So we have to assume that Dancer knows both Warren and Billy," Renee said. "And we're going to assume that the Billy in the letter is you. How do you think he knows you're here? Involved with the case?"

"There were a lot of cameras shooting coverage as we entered and left the Gemini Ballroom," Billy said. "That's the only way anyone would know that I'm here. I've been in Seattle for less than a week."

"Have you met up with anyone? Set up drinks with friends? Is there some other way for Dancer to know you're in Seattle?" Renee asked. "Your new hire announcement hasn't been released by HR yet." She glared at him as if that was his fault.

Halley snickered quietly to herself. Probably Billy had put off meeting with them. She knew she would.

"No, ma'am," Billy said. "I don't have that many friends left here."

"What about family?" Renee said.

"My mother knows I'm coming to Seattle, but she doesn't actually know when I'm supposed to arrive," Billy said.

Interesting. Seemed that Billy didn't have a very good relationship with his relatives.

"Billy didn't call any of us," Warren said after a moment. "I met with Marcus and Peter at the club last week. Your name never even came up," he added accusingly.

Billy shrugged. Halley could see how acutely embarrassed he was. She remembered reading that his mother had money, enough for him to attend some fancy academy high school.

"Where does Dancer know you two from?" Renee asked.

"Probably high school, right?" Warren said.

Phoenix nodded, then caught Halley's eye and nodded again.

Interesting. Had Marc (the original alter ego of Phoenix) also gone to school with Billy and Warren? Roxy had implied that Phoenix had a lot of money.

"This is good," Dick said, smacking his hand together. "Now we're getting somewhere. Billy, you and Warren should go through your high school yearbook. Pick out who might be a suspect." He paused, then added, "We have another connection to the killer through the SBDM community," Dick said.

"BDSM," Billy corrected.

"Whatever. Who was into that kind of thing? The freaks, the outcasts? Look through your yearbook. See if some memory pops up. This could be our first real break," Dick said.

Phoenix shook their head as if they wanted to disagree. "Not a good idea?" Halley whispered.

"Not our year," they said.

That confirmed that all of them had a high school connection. And that Phoenix was concerned that it was someone who they all knew.

"And you're now off the case," Renee said to Billy. She held up her hand, not wanting to hear any of his excuses. "It's not because of you. You know that, right? It's because of the lawyers at the other end, when we finally catch this bastard. I don't want to give them any leverage."

Billy sighed and shook his head, finally saying, "Yes, ma'am."

Halley knew he didn't like it. But Renee was right. Billy couldn't be involved if there was a chance that his connections could jeopardize the case.

"All right, then," Renee said. "We have access to most

yearbooks online. See if you can find your killer there. And good luck," she added before she swept from the room.

"You heard her," Dick told Billy. "Go get 'em, tiger."

"Fine," Billy said. He turned to Warren. "Want to step over to my desk? See what we can find in the way of yearbooks online?"

Warren smiled at Billy as if Billy had just offered him a glass of fucking Bud Lite.

"At your service," was all he said. The pair of them wandered off.

Dick suddenly stepped into the meeting room. "I suppose you heard that," he said sourly.

"Heard what, officer?" Phoenix asked, using their beautiful voice to its full advantage to soothe Dick's feathers.

"This room has been double-booked," Dick growled in return. "Seems we'll be using interrogation room number two instead."

Phoenix rose and followed Dick, walking in a way that reminded Halley of the most beautiful women who knew they looked good and took their time walking into a room, always making an entrance.

She'd read about classes intended for straight women, taught by drag queens, in how to do makeup as well as how to walk in heels.

If she ever decided she wanted to change her appearance, she would have to look into those.

In the meanwhile, it was time to face the music.

CHAPTER 15

HALLEY'S STOMACH was growling loudly by the time they'd finished answering Dick's questions. She was still astonished that he'd agreed to question the pair of them together, instead of separating them. She wasn't a lawyer, she had no legal grounds for demanding that she stay with Phoenix.

Though Dick, as well as everyone in the department, had gone through sensitivity training, it did occur to her that the reason Dick had wanted her in the room was to act as a buffer to Phoenix, especially since he'd just lost Billy.

Dick hadn't gotten any new information out of Phoenix, nothing that Halley hadn't been able to ascertain on her own.

The pair of them stood on the sidewalk outside of the downtown police precinct. The wan November sun barely made its way through the clouds. Winds howled down the street. The constant traffic made a good substitute for the sound of the waves on the shore behind them.

"Now what?" Phoenix asked. They'd already called for an Uber to take them to their next destination. Halley had declined a ride. Since she was already downtown, might as well follow Mr. Farrow to his usual lunch.

Halley shrugged in response. "There really isn't much else

we can do. Unless you want to go looking through high school yearbook pictures as well."

Phoenix pressed their brightly painted lips together, then shook their head. "I already have my suspicions. And thank you for not bringing that up to the dick."

"You're welcome," Halley said. Though she'd felt uncomfortable about leaving that detail out, telling Dick that Phoenix had some suspicions wouldn't have helped.

"You should follow Warren," Phoenix said.

"The cops will be doing that," Halley said. "I don't want to get in the way of their investigation."

"They'll fuck it up," Phoenix said bluntly.

"And if I were around, they'd blame me for it," Halley replied. "I would just as soon that they fuck it up on their own time, thank you very much."

"Warren's a dead man walking," Phoenix declared.

"Why do you say that?" Halley asked.

"His ego won't allow him to let go of this," Phoenix said. "He'll deliberately lose his police escort. And Dancer will take him."

Halley shook her head, not following Phoenix's logic.

"Dancer doesn't plan on giving Warren an interview. Warren will be their next kill."

Halley shrugged. "We don't know that, not for certain. Plus there isn't anything I can do. If Warren deliberately slips his police escort, that's on his head."

"Fine," Phoenix said, waving at the car that was obviously their ride. "Let him be the victim of his own stupidity. Just call me Cassandra. Remember?"

With that, they slid into the car, the driver rejoining traffic immediately.

Halley sighed, frustrated. There were so many arguments against her doing something as idiotic as following an individual that the police were already tailing. She couldn't even begin to enumerate them.

Plus, she had other work to do. Investigative work that was actually paying her bills. In addition to the Farrow case, she had two others that she needed to put in some time on.

She hunched her shoulders together against the blast of cold wind that came rolling down the street as she walked up toward Pioneer Square. Honestly, there wasn't anything she could do, short of kidnapping Warren herself.

However, as she sipped her soup and watched the probably innocent Mr. Farrow eat his own lunch, she wondered just how prophetic Phoenix would turn out to be.

HALLEY SPENT the rest of Wednesday and all day Thursday working her other cases. The one from the Mazikowski family was particularly interesting.

Mr. Mazikowski had three children from his first wife. She'd died young, breast cancer, and he had raised the three kids himself. After the last had gone off to college, he'd started dating again, and eventually, met and married another woman, Dorothy Loretto. She also had three children, from her first husband, though they'd been divorced.

Though Mr. Mazikowski's children tried to stay in touch with him, it wasn't easy, as Mr. Mazikowski and his new wife were snowbirds, and only spent half their time in Seattle, the rest down in Arizona. As they had an RV to travel between the two homes, they would frequently "take the long way" as his son had said, spending a month or more on the road.

As Mr. Mazikowski didn't believe in cell phones, that made communication even more difficult. They would call Mr. Mazikowski's new wife now and again, though she didn't care much for talking to them. Still, the children worked at it, mostly, when their own lives didn't interfere.

It took them a while to piece together the news that none of them had heard from their dad in a while. During the summer, they just figured that he was on the road, traveling.

Fall came, and still no word. They started to grow worried. Particularly when they got no answer when they tried calling their stepmother, and their mail started getting returned.

None of the children had the ability to travel to Seattle: between the approaching holidays and young children of their own, they couldn't make it happen.

Instead, they'd reached out to Halley.

It took her a few days of solid digging, but her hunch had paid off: Both the elder Mr. Mazikowski and his new wife had died in a car accident earlier that spring. The local children had been on hand to take care of all the arrangements.

Which included selling all the property and goods, then splitting the money between the three of them, never reaching out to the step siblings.

It was all perfectly legal, as far as Halley could tell. Mr. Mazikowski's will had left everything to his new wife, and then to his surviving children. As the new Mrs. Mazikowski had survived her husband by several days (the doctors had thought she'd make it, but then she'd contacted pneumonia and had declined rapidly), her will had taken effect, and only her children had inherited.

Could the surviving children make a court case for being cut out of the inheritance? For not being told that their father had been killed? For having to wait until their letters started being returned? Yes. Would they win? Maybe, and only after a lot of expense, aggravation, and time.

Halley had a video conference call with her clients,

spelling out her findings, before she mailed them all the evidence.

There wasn't much else she could do for them, except to assure them that she was willing to testify in court as to her findings if it came to that.

After they hung up, Halley sat for a while in the conference room. The nice weather had finally broken, and it was pissing down rain again. Snow had already been reported in the hills. Looked as though this was going to be yet another hard, cold winter.

Halley carefully filed her papers and stood, stretching. She'd gone to the Krav Maga dojo the previous night, finding it fulfilling to take out her aggression on the mat, though she sported more than a few bruises that day.

Tonight she'd take yet another long hot soak in her bathtub. Maybe she'd call Taylor as well, see if she wanted to get a quiet drink after dinner, something more to loosen Halley up.

A text came in as Halley was leaving the conference room.

It was from Phoenix.

Warren is missing.

CHAPTER 16

DANCER WAITED JUST inside the door of the empty warehouse, watching Warren on the remote screen. Though Dancer had instructed Warren to not bring any electronics or tracking devices, they were certain that Warren had disobeyed.

That was all right. Dancer would teach him about the need for discipline.

Warren waited, as he'd been told. Doing what he'd been instructed to do.

Ah, they never admitted it at first. But they all would place themselves under Dancer's control in the end.

Warren had at least come alone, as he'd been instructed.

Dancer understood that Warren had done as he'd been told because he smelled the potential money. His news agency would have exclusive rights to any interview Dancer gave. Warren could then slice and dice it a hundred different ways, selling different segments to the various agencies.

It was a story he might be able to milk for millions.

Not that Warren was desperate for money. No, he just wanted more. Like that junky hit of cocaine.

Dancer watched, amused. It was better to meet here,

away from Dancer's abode. Fortunately, Dancer had already planned on how to get rid of Warren's car.

Just a few more moments. Stretch Warren's patience as thin as it could go.

Then let the games begin.

CHAPTER 17

"REMIND me why we're doing this again?" Halley asked as she drove across the 520 bridge Friday morning.

"Jennifer Strauss has agreed to talk with us," Phoenix said from the passenger seat. They were a little more somberly dressed that day, and actually had their arms covered for the first time, in a black jacket that fit snugly over their ample breasts. They wore baggy women's pants that had a subtly gray stripe, as well as huge black platform shoes.

It had surprised Halley that Phoenix wasn't wearing a silver pump, something to offset the black. When Phoenix noticed Halley looking at their outfit, they finally said, "I'm wearing black for mourning. You know that Warren is dead, right? That he went to meet Dancer alone?"

Halley gulped. "There wasn't anything I could have done to prevent that," she said defensively.

"I know, child." Phoenix sighed and looked out the window at the gray water speeding by. "There wasn't anything anyone could have done."

"Why aren't the police interviewing Mrs. Strauss?" Halley asked.

"They already did. Yesterday," Phoenix assured her. "So you don't have to worry about poisoning the well, or some such nonsense."

"Thanks," Halley said dryly. She wasn't looking forward to interviewing a potentially grieving widow.

How had Phoenix managed the interview? Had they used their high school connection?

"Tell me what you can about Jennifer Strauss," Halley suggested.

"Trophy wife," Phoenix said. "Committed to doing charitable works. As well as looking good on camera."

"Did you go to school with her as well?" Halley had to ask.

"No, she grew up in Colorado," Phoenix said. "Met Warren at another friend's wedding. According to them, it was a love match. More like a 'love money' match."

"What do you mean?" Halley said.

"Jennifer had her own money coming into this marriage. Money that Warren used to buy his news station," Phoenix said. "Never forget that. Money is always drawn to more money. It was what Dancer used to entice Warren. The possibility of more money from the interview."

How did Phoenix know that? Had it been because they, too, had come from money?

Halley exited the freeway, then off the main drag and into the winding streets. Phoenix pointed out their turn when it arrived. Jennifer and Warren Strauss lived in a gated community south of Kirkland. The gate was open when they drove up. Was that standard? Would it be open during daylight hours? Or was it normally locked? Halley made a note to check.

A narrow road wound its way through the subdivision, with large speed bumps running across it to slow cars down.

Immaculate, broad yards ran from the street up to the mansions. All of them had three car garages, many with additional large ports holding motorhomes or boats.

The houses were all at least faced with brick, as well as two or three stories tall. They weren't identical, but similar enough to fit together, make a cohesive neighborhood. Bare trees grew near the houses, probably flowering cherries that would look beautiful come spring. Trimmed boxwood hedges separated one property from the next, maybe three foot tall, so that while the neighbors weren't sharing space, they could always compare lawns.

A series of cul-de-sacs ran off the main road. Jennifer and Warren Strauss lived in one toward the back of the neighborhood, past most of the other houses. It was a somber, brown brick building with both a three car garage on the left side as well as a large boat awning.

"Did you grow up in a place like this?" Halley asked as she parked her car in the driveway.

Phoenix shook their head, then said with a grin, "Nope. Someplace much richer. Old money. Not new."

Halley merely nodded and filed that away as yet another piece of information to add to the puzzle of Phoenix.

Jennifer Strauss met them at the door. She was tall, at least five foot eight, Caucasian, mid-thirties, with a long face and long brown hair that she wore tucked behind her ears. Bony wrists stuck out from the off-white cardigan she wore. She still had the perfect summer tan, probably from a booth, not a bottle. She wore white pearl earrings that matched her necklace. Under the cardigan she wore a somber brown blouse. Darker brown slacks covered her long legs.

Halley hated herself for immediately jumping to the conclusion that Mrs. Strauss had dressed that way so she'd look good on camera. Solid colors. No designs or stripes.

But she also knew that she might be right.

"Hi, I'm Halley Brown, a private investigator, and this is Phoenix," Halley said as way of introduction. "You said that you would talk with us? About Warren?"

Jennifer nodded. She glanced at Phoenix, did a double take, blinked, then shook her head, seemingly in disbelief. "Have you found him? Is he dead?"

Fear filled her tone.

"He's still just missing," Halley said gently. Damn it! Had Phoenix somehow implied to Jennifer that they were with the cops?

The front hallway had a grand staircase on the left, curving around and leading to a balcony. It was perfect for making an entrance. Jennifer led them to the right, through the open living room to the kitchen. Windows filled the walls, showing the yard and the neighbor's house, as well as providing all the light.

Jennifer went to stand behind the island in the kitchen, picking up her coffee mug though not drinking it. The way she wrapped her hands around it made Halley think she just wanted the warmth.

The kitchen seemed cold. Maybe it was the fake marble countertops that were colored black and brown. Maybe it was the dark brown wood cupboards, and the black and stainless all new appliances.

Or maybe it was because the place was spotless. No one cooked here. They catered when they entertained. Halley would bet that the fridge only contained energy drinks, the latest designer cream for their coffee, and maybe some yogurt.

"When did you last hear from Warren?" Halley asked, setting her phone to record. She stayed on "her" side of the kitchen island, respecting Mrs. Strauss' space. If she needed to lean into the woman, she could cross the divide later.

"Wednesday morning," Jennifer said. "We were both on our way out. He said he'd be home for dinner."

"Out?" Halley asked.

Jennifer nodded. "I had an appointment with my tennis instructor. Then lunch with friends. I told him I'd be home for dinner as well." She sighed, her stare growing glassy. "I don't remember if I told him I loved him. I'm sure I didn't."

Halley wasn't sure if her grief was an act or real. She'd certainly already told all of this to the police already. Probably just rehearsing the speech again for the eventual cameras. "Did you talk with him after that?"

"No," Jennifer said. "I was busy. So was he. That's normal for us. We try to talk in person, not on the phone."

She absentmindedly took a sip of her coffee, then looked up, horrified. "I'm sorry," she said. "I should have offered you some. What was I thinking?" She couldn't have them thinking that she might be a bad hostess.

"We don't need anything, darling," Phoenix said gently, their voice as soothing as a warm blanket. "Tell us about the rest of your day."

Jennifer reeled off her appointments: after lunch, she went to see her manicurist, then had meeting with a charity organization. She'd decided she didn't want to go out to eat that night, so she had their on-call chef come in and fix dinner.

"Were you surprised when Warren didn't come home that night?" Halley said.

Jennifer frowned. It appeared to be her most natural face, not the pleasant smile she'd been trying to maintain through the interview. "Yes and no. He worked late some nights. And sometimes the boys called and they went out. But we had an agreement. He was supposed to call before he went to tie one on."

"Did he break the agreement often?" Halley said, already knowing the answer.

"All the damned time," Jennifer said. A touch of heat entered her voice. "He was always sorry, but then he'd go and do it again. So I really wasn't worried that he didn't show up. A little pissed off, but not worried." She paused, then added, "But then he didn't call the next morning. He always called the next morning to apologize."

"What did you do Wednesday evening?" Halley asked, watching her closely.

Jennifer sighed. "I was home alone," she said. "I know, I know. No one can vouch for my whereabouts," she added. "Except that you can check the records with the front gate. You'll see that I didn't leave."

Halley took a note. "So the gate is always supposed to be closed?" she asked.

"Only at night. It's open during the day."

After they reached the end of their questions, Halley asked if they could look around some.

"Sure. You want to see Warren's study?" Jennifer offered.

"That would be lovely," Phoenix told her graciously.

Jennifer led them them back the way they'd come, toward the front door, then around the other side, to a hallway that ran under the front stairs. "The layout of this place is nice sometimes, a pain in the ass other times," she complained.

They passed a guest bedroom and a full bathroom before reaching Warren's study.

Halley shook her head when she looked in. It was a stereotypical "man cave" complete with a mini-fridge that she was certain was full of beer. Pennants from Seattle University hung behind the desk. The whole room was done in dark leather. A huge desk took up one third of the room, covered with stacks of paper, magazines, and files. A smaller computer monitor took up one corner. The ergonomic chair behind the desk was an architectural marvel, and it probably cost more than three months of Halley's income. A long, low credenza rested against the far wall. Pictures were scattered across the top of it, probably placed there by Jennifer, not by Warren. The wall opposite the desk held four large TV screens, probably so Warren could run several news channels side by side, catching up on the competition.

Though Jennifer had turned on the overhead light, the room still seemed dark. Halley very carefully didn't touch anything as she made her way over to the window, looking out through the slats.

The view from Warren's office included the side yard, blocked on one side by the back of the garage. A covered deck ran from the house to the garage, a place where Warren could enjoy a few brewskies while just hanging out.

The file cabinets were all locked, of course. Halley suspected that Jennifer wouldn't have a key. The locked safe that stood hidden by the desk didn't have a key, but instead, a combination lock as well as a thumbprint scanner.

Nothing seemed out of order in the study. No hastily scrawled notes. Nothing looked missing or out of place.

After a few more minutes, Halley and Phoenix followed Jennifer back to the front of the house.

"We'll let you know if we hear anything," Phoenix assured Jennifer, taking both of her hands in theirs. "You hang in there."

Jennifer seemed a bit bedazzled by Phoenix. She blinked and gave a bleary smile, before stepping back into the cold, empty house and firmly locking the door.

Halley and Phoenix looked at each other and shrugged. They stayed where they were, pausing to look around the neighborhood. The view was nice. Neighbor's houses with beautiful yards. A sameness that some would find comforting. Gray clouds gathered overhead, but the rain had paused for a while.

Next to the garage stood a boat shelter. *News Worthy* was painted on the side of the boat. Figured. Warren would consider any of his appearances to be worthy of news. Halley rolled her eyes and started walking toward the car.

Then she froze.

Phoenix was saying something. Halley couldn't hear them.

Instead, Halley walked back up the driveway studying the boat.

The front of the boat cover flapped in the wind.

No matter how lazy Warren might be, he knew better than to leave a boat uncovered for the winter.

Halley looked around. Nothing else seemed out of place.

No, wait.

What was a ladder doing there? Resting on the garage door?

Unless the Strauss' were having work done, they would never leave equipment laying out like that. It just wasn't done. Once the workers were finished, they were supposed to vanish without a trace.

"Do you see what I'm seeing?" Halley asked Phoenix.

Phoenix looked at the boat, then back at Halley.

Halley slowly walked over toward the boat, pulling on her driving gloves. Phoenix followed several steps behind and to the side, as if not wanting to be drawn in too close to the drama.

Could Halley see over the gunnel of the boat without climbing up? No.

She looked at Phoenix, who nodded at her. Halley's legs were long enough and her balance was good enough that she could step onto the fender of the trailer holding the boat, then pop her head up over the side, without touching the boat itself.

"Oh, Jesus," Halley said as she stepped back down, stumbling away. Her stomach recoiled, and her breakfast threatened to make a reappearance.

Phoenix took one look at Halley's face. "I'm guessing we know where Warren ended up."

CHAPTER 18

HALLEY COULDN'T GET the image of Warren's surprised look out of her head. His eyes were wide open. A red ball-gag held his mouth open. His hands were splayed open, tied in place with only a couple of fancy knots. It appeared that Dancer had improvised, using plain white rope they'd found on the boat instead of bringing their own bright red cord.

The other details that Halley tried to gloss over were just as bad. Warren had been made up to look like a clown. His nose had been extended to a sharp point, the tip painted bright red. White makeup had been applied to his face, with red dots on his cheeks. His lips had also been painted red, a huge smear around the gag.

Warren laid on his side, legs curled up, as if doing some sort of twisting stretch. Sticking out of his anus was a huge black cock/dildo. It was bigger than Halley's forearm. Blood covered the area.

Whip marks covered Warren's torso. They would be recent, from the last day or so though they weren't bleeding. Blood did drip from Warren's penis, pierced with two long, curved needles.

There wasn't an obvious cause of death, unless Warren

had bled to death. Chances were, though, that Dancer had killed Warren, then continued to play with the body.

Halley called Dick, let him know the news. Phoenix agreed to stay outside with the body, while Halley drew the short straw and went back to the house to tell the wife.

Jennifer knew something was wrong after taking one look at Halley's face.

"You've found him. He's dead. Where is he? Where did you find him?" Jennifer asked.

She looked around wildly, spotting Phoenix standing next to the boat, talking on their phone.

"Is he here? Was he killed here?" Jennifer shrieked.

Halley caught her before she could run out of the house and over to the boat.

"No," Halley said firmly. "Listen to me. Listen to me," she said, holding onto the widow's arm, shaking it, trying to get Jennifer to focus on her instead.

"You do not want to see him like that," Halley told her. "That should not be your final image of your husband. Wait until we get him cleaned up. Trust me. Wait."

Jennifer didn't appear to understand what Halley was saying at first. Finally, she gulped. Tears streamed down her face. "It's…it's that bad?" she said, her voice broken.

"Just wait," Halley told her. "Let's go inside."

The will seemed to run out of Jennifer and she meekly let Halley lead her back into the house. They sat down on the uncomfortable couch in the living room. On the way there, Halley snagged a designer's box of tissues and put them on the low coffee table for Jennifer.

"Is he, did he die quickly?" Jennifer asked. Her eyes seemed glazed over again.

"We won't know that until the ME performs an autopsy," Halley said. "He probably didn't suffer much," she added. Technically she was telling the truth. Since Warren had disappeared Wednesday night, Dancer hadn't been able to "play" with him for long.

"Is there someone you can call? Someone who can come sit with you?" Halley asked.

Jennifer nodded, then pointed silently over her shoulder to the kitchen counter.

Halley went and fetched Jennifer's phone, not taking offense at the silent command. She knew that Jennifer was just reverting to type, who she was underneath the appearance she put on for everyone else: a spoiled rich kid used to getting her way.

Halley made them both some coffee. The espresso machine had more buttons and programming capabilities than the first lunar rocket.

Jennifer called her mother. She wept openly on the phone.

Then she called a girlfriend, who promised to be there right away.

Halley wondered if the girlfriend would call a publicist before putting in an appearance.

Jennifer joined Halley in the kitchen as she finished pouring the coffee. "We were waiting to have kids," she said. "Just another year. Then we were going to start raising our family. I'm younger than Warren. We had time. Just another year."

Halley silently handed her the coffee. She'd wondered at the size of the house, with it just being Jennifer and Warren. The neighborhood seemed set up for people with children.

"What can you tell me about Warren's work?" Halley asked. She didn't know if talking about Warren would help Jennifer or hurt. But she'd figured that it would be easier if she talked to Jennifer while Phoenix stayed with the body.

"He had a corporate position in media," Jennifer assured her. "He owned one of the local TV stations. They were affiliated with an international brand. But Warren still owned the station, free and clear."

The pride that filled her voice surprised Halley. Maybe it had been more than just a "love money" match. Then again, maybe it was just the pride of ownership.

Halley sat with Jennifer until her friend arrived. She pulled in just as the CSI unit arrived. Uniformed officers were already on hand, stringing tape all the way around the scene and keeping onlookers to the street. Then Halley went back outside to stand guard with Phoenix until Dick could arrive.

"Why aren't there more news vans?" Halley asked. Wouldn't the police converging on Warren Strauss' property guarantee coverage?

Phoenix pouted at her. "Seems that having a gated community means that you can actually shut the gate sometimes."

"Too bad. You'd look great on camera," Halley said. She studied Phoenix for a moment.

Crap. Phoenix was in solid colors as well. Had they done that on purpose? So that they would record well?

Had they already known that the body would be there?

Halley kept her suspicions to herself as Dick bore down on them. "What in the hell are you two doing here?" he demanded.

Phoenix drew themselves up to their full height. "Your job," they said simply. "You were already here, yesterday. You didn't notice the boat. She did."

Dick's attention turned from Phoenix to Halley. The heat from his glare was almost physical.

"What did you see?" he said.

Halley described the situation as well as she could, how the flapping of the boat cover had drawn her attention. She also pointed out the ladder that hadn't been put away.

"So your partner here didn't point out the boat to you?" Dick said.

Obviously, he'd come to the same suspicion that Phoenix was somehow involved with Dancer.

"No, they did not," Halley said. For better or worse, Phoenix was their partner in this. At least for the time being.

There really wasn't anything else that Halley and Phoenix could tell Dick. They agreed to come back down to the precinct later that afternoon to give their statements.

Only when they were back in the car did Halley ask the one question she really had.

"Was Warren a clown?" she asked. "Like the class clown?"

Phoenix shook their head. "He wasn't the class clown," they said. "But he wasn't the most studious, either."

"The other bodies weren't wearing makeup like that," Halley said driving away slowly.

"True, but they were all staged in various extravagant positions," Phoenix said. "This kill was more improvised. Not as planned out as the previous ones."

Halley nodded. That was probably true.

"So how do we stop Dancer?" she asked. "Before they kill again?"

"Oh, honey, if I knew that, do you think I'd be here, riding with you? Not that you aren't delightfully butch," Phoenix said.

Halley rolled her eyes at that.

"What would you do if you were working the case?" Phoenix asked.

"I'd have a hell of a lot of reports to write," Halley said lightly. But she couldn't actually trivialize what had just happened. "I'd also have a lot more data to be sifting through. Maybe other leads to be following. Maybe CSI could come up with a fingerprint or some other data about Dancer."

"Dancer wouldn't be that careless," Phoenix said.

"You know that Dick and the others are probably considering you to be a suspect at this point," Halley pointed out.

"I know," Phoenix said. They gave a putout sigh. "They already consider me a deviant. But I believe I have alibis for this latest kill, at least. They wouldn't even try to charge me, I don't think."

Halley nodded. The cops were likely to be a bit gun shy when it came to making an arrest in this case. While the brass were probably chewing Dick's ass to catch the killer, they were also, at the same time, happy for the caution.

"So who would you go and interview next?" Halley asked. "You said you had your suspicions."

Phoenix pressed their lips together tightly for a few moments before nodding. "You want to go on another drive tomorrow? Maybe go and stake out a different house?"

"Sure," Halley said. She could rearrange the meetings she had in the afternoon.

When Phoenix didn't say anything more, she asked, "Where?"

"My old stomping grounds."

CHAPTER 19

Dancer pouted as they watched the news.

They'd known that Warren lived in a gated community. They'd driven there themselves, depositing the body. In Warren's car. There had been a certain lovely symmetry in that.

But then the cops had closed the gate! Locked the press out!

Someone needed to have a *word* with the police about freedom of information. How some news was just more important than the rest of the tripe the newscasters were always spouting.

The police just weren't releasing any of the good bits. Now the newscasts were going on and on and fucking *on* about Warren and what a good man he'd been, such a responsible and upstanding citizen.

Even the press conference held by the police hadn't delivered anything good. Just a community search for who had seen Warren last, any information about the killer.

Dancer was tempted to troll the hotline, but knew it really wouldn't give them any satisfaction.

No one knew about Dancer. Dancer lived in the shadows, out of line of sight from the rest of society. But Dancer still longed to be *seen*, for the art in their very soul to be pierced by the bright light of day.

It wasn't a contradiction to Dancer. It was just their nature as an artist.

Dancer lived for every detail the talking heads did give out, reveling in the fear that now pinched every voice. Men like Warren were supposed to be *safe* from the monsters under the bed. Not fall victim to them.

When the police press conference was finished, Dancer sighed, disgusted. While Dancer would admit that the installation of Warren's body hadn't been as inspired as the previous boy, it didn't mean their art shouldn't be appreciated.

Dancer had had to improvise, as all good artists would.

The clown makeup had been truly inspired. How Warren had wept as Dancer had painted his true image on his face.

Dancer had finally gotten impatient with Warren's crying, and had given him something to cry about, as their mother had often threatened.

Using the ropes on the boat hadn't been necessary. Dancer had brought their own ropes. There was just something about being in the moment and using what was on hand.

Maybe for their next MO, Dancer would challenge themselves to use implements in their immediate surrounding for the kill.

That could provide some interesting artwork. Spontaneous.

Yes. Dancer couldn't wait to get started with their new life. They hadn't found the perfect spot yet, but they would. Something would speak to them as they drove out of state, into the sunset, as it were.

They just had to finish the business here first. One last kill that would free Dancer. Allow them to spread their wings and truly fly.

Find a new place to practice their art.

CHAPTER 20

WITHOUT THINKING ABOUT IT, Halley answered the call from her sister. She was back in her condo, listening to the evening news about Warren. She took the time to memorize the license plate number for his car, in case she saw it tomorrow on the stakeout with Phoenix.

"Mom fell. Again," Caroline said, starting off the conversation with a bang, as usual.

Halley sighed and shook her head. "How bad is it?" She didn't want to have to go back out to Spokane, wouldn't, in fact, unless her mother was actually at death's door.

"She cracked a couple of ribs this time," Caroline said.

"There's not much they can do for cracked ribs," Halley pointed out.

"I know! Don't think I don't know. I told them that they needed to hospitalize her—it's the only way to get her sober. But they wouldn't. Wouldn't even bandage them. Just told her to be careful and be on her way," Caroline said, sounding disgusted.

"Did they prescribe painkillers for her?" Halley asked as she got up from her desk, walking toward the front windows. The trees were all bare now, what with the wind and the rain this last week. The brilliant yellow and red leaves scattered along the edges of the street were starting to fade as well. The neighbors up the way had already broken out their Christmas lights, the outline of their house lit up in red and white, with glowing red and white candy canes in the front windows.

It still wasn't enough to cheer up Halley's dark mood.

The radiator under the window began to hiss. Great. It would be a sauna in here in less than an hour.

"Of course, they prescribed pain killers," Caroline said, her disgust amplifying. "Mom insisted. Fortunately, I was the one who picked up the scrip. Told Mom that they'd run out."

"But you still filled it, didn't you?" Halley said.

"I had to! Mom said she needed them," Caroline said, not understanding just how contradictory her report was being.

Halley knew better than to ask what Caroline was doing with the pills. Besides taking them herself, now.

It was one of the reasons why Halley only went out drinking with Taylor once a week and never kept any alcohol in her condo. Never took any prescription pills, either. There was just too good of a chance that she'd get addicted to something, particularly given her family history. Despite how little she physically or emotionally resembled the rest of her family.

"Well, at least Mom can't get up in the middle of the night to fetch herself a drink," Halley said.

"She did anyway. I found a bottle of vodka stashed under the bathroom sink," Caroline said. "I'd wondered why she'd been taking so long in there."

Halley grimaced. She didn't bother reminding Caroline that she also needed to check under the old-fashioned clawfoot bathtub for bottles. Or behind the tub. Or hidden as a bottle of shampoo. Or any of the other creative places that their mother had stashed her alcohol since moving in with Caroline and being told that she couldn't drink so much anymore, not in front of the boys.

"There isn't anything we can do if she doesn't want to get sober," Halley said.

"But if you were here, you could watch her as well," Caroline said.

"And as soon as I left, she'd go back to it. You know she isn't about to quit." Halley opened up the window and stuck a small dowel rod under it to keep the heavy glass open a fraction. Then she walked around the room and set up her fans.

"You don't know that," Caroline said. "She always liked you better. She might listen to you."

Halley rolled her eyes. She wasn't about to get drawn into that argument again. "She needs to decide for herself that enough is enough. Neither of us can say or do anything."

"So you would just have me abandon our own mother?" Caroline said, her voice rising to a dramatic pitch.

"Yes," Halley snapped. "Yes, I would. Let her die in her own piss and vomit. I'm tired of trying to take care of someone who's determined to die."

"What in your selfish little life could be more important than your mother?"

"Oh, I don't know. Maybe stopping a killer? Saving someone's life?"

"You wish," Caroline said dismissively. "You aren't even a cop anymore."

"Fuck you," Halley said. She'd gotten enough of that this afternoon when she'd gone down to the precinct to give her statement, fully reamed out by both Dick and Renee. She wasn't sure what treatment Phoenix had received, and at this point, she didn't care.

"Don't lie to me and tell me that you're doing something worthwhile there in Seattle. You're just there because you were always the favorite. You never had to stay and clean up your messes," Caroline continued, building up a good head of steam. "While I did."

"I don't remember that, actually," Halley said. "I don't think that was how it happened at all. I think instead I decided to make something of myself while the rest of you miserable fuckers insisted on staying in that hell hole of a small town and wallowing in your own shit."

"You miserable cunt!" Caroline screamed. "How dare you suggest that you're better than the rest of us? How about you come and walk a mile in my shoes for once instead of being all superior?"

"No, thank you," Halley said. "I have too much self-respect to be a martyr that way."

"Fuck you," Caroline said.

"No, fuck you," Halley said as she swiped off the phone. She found herself shaking with anger.

Goddamn it! Only her sister could get under her skin that way. Halley had not been the favorite. She'd just applied herself, actually worked when she was in school, cared about getting good grades as well as getting the hell out of Spokane.

Halley strode around her tiny living room once, twice, before she stopped herself. She was pacing like a trapped wild animal.

She was not trapped. Not like her sister. Not like her mother.

She texted Taylor, seeing if she could go out for a drink.

The instant reply soothed Halley. They quickly arranged to meet at one of the bars on Twelfth, between Pike and Pine.

Halley grabbed her leather jacket and steamed out of her condo. The night air would help calm her temper.

And the beer she was looking forward to would be the

only one she'd drink tonight, because goddamn it she wasn't about to turn out to be like her mother or sister.

***

HALLEY TOOK the long way down to the bar, as Taylor wouldn't be there for thirty minutes. She walked past Twelfth, up to Broadway, then down. The construction for the buildings above the new light rail station was ongoing. She crossed the street, not wanting to walk in the closed-in walkway provided by the construction barriers. The huge crane that sat in the middle of the chaos had a brilliant green Christmas tree at the top of it.

Many of the shops were already decorated for Christmas, with plenty of lights and pine boughs in their front windows. The rain has passed, leaving the streets wet, but another storm was brewing based on the strong winds that whipped down the street, pressing against Halley's back, making her hurry forward.

Students sauntered from one building to the next, taking their time and filling the street. Though it was Friday night, the sidewalks weren't yet filled with partiers and tourists.

Halley passed one shop that was actually decorated for Thanksgiving, with a huge turkey painted across the front window. Her phone buzzed just a moment later.

Text message from Caroline. Fuck if she was going to answer it tonight. Knowing her luck, her sister would be uninviting her for Thanksgiving. Halley hadn't been looking forward to it too much, though she would miss seeing her nephews.

Halley angrily turned up Pike, walking back toward Twelfth. She passed the Gemini Ballroom, which was advertising that it would be open again the following week. God, all the bodies had been found close to this area. The black box theatre where the first one had been found was up on Twelfth. The little art house was down on Pine. And now the Gemini.

Did Dancer actually live in the neighborhood? Or was this just their dumping ground? Halley felt it was the latter. Had they gone to the community college here, though? Or even Seattle University? Was that why they were comfortable with Capitol Hill?

Halley slowed as she walked up the hill, toward the East Precinct. She didn't feel intimidated by the cops. Not exactly. She just felt unsettled, between her sister and the nasty conversations she'd had with Dick that afternoon.

She didn't belong there, with the cops. She'd known that for a while. She liked the work she did as a private investigator, though there were few crimes to solve. Just muck to rake through, discovering the sordid details of people's lives.

Halley couldn't say afterwards what set her radar off. Maybe it was because she was nearing the police station and that put her on her guard. Maybe it was something in the crowds around her that made her step to the side, closer to the street. Maybe there had been the smell of gasoline that caught her attention.

Whatever it was, she found her attention locked on a car parked in a no parking zone. What kind of stupid tourist would leave their car there, in front of the station? That was just begging for a ticket.

Wait a second.

Halley hated that feeling that crept over her shoulders as it dawned on her that she recognized the car. Or rather, the make and model.

As well as the license plate.

That was Warren's car.

Shit.

Crap.

Halley ran up to the car. Whoever was in the passenger seat was slumped over.

Was that Dancer's next victim? Were they already dead?

Halley raced into the precinct. "Help!" she said to the intake officer. "That car that's currently illegally parked in front of the building belongs to Warren Strauss. And there's a body in the front seat."

"What car?" the officer asked. She was a young African American woman, probably just out of the police academy. She wore her hair in a wild afro, decorated with cute red ribbons. Her nametag proclaimed her as R. Damask.

Halley pointed. "You need to call Detective Dick Wilkerson. Let him know."

"Shit," Officer Damask replied.

"Do you have a slimjim? A sharp rock? Anything to break the window with?" Halley asked. She knew that Dick and the rest would read her the riot act for disturbing their crime scene. But possibly the person in the front seat wasn't dead.

"No, ma'am," Officer Damask said. "You need to stay away from the vehicle." She was already calling it in.

Halley looked outside. A skinny man in a dress, with a long beard and hair, was bending over next to the car. He appeared to be putting a flier under the windshield wiper.

"Hey!" Halley called, racing back outside. "Get away from there!"

The man glanced over his shoulder at Halley, then let go of the windshield wiper with a snap.

Halley didn't understand what happened next. She was racing toward the car. Then the next minute, she was on her ass twenty feet away. All she heard was a loud ringing sound. The world seemed to waver. She'd been on her way someplace. But where?

She struggled to his feet. People were nearby, trying to

talk with her. She couldn't hear them. Couldn't understand what they were saying. She had to go see the car.

What car, though?

It took Halley three tries before she started moving back up the sidewalk, toward the corner where the precinct was.

Toward the monstrous bonfire that now burned in the street, where a car had once been parked.

CHAPTER 21

DANCER STOOD in the street with the rest of the crowd, hanging out near the still smoldering car on Capitol Hill. The cops had cordoned off the entire intersection fairly quickly, pushing Dancer and the others back.

At least they weren't the only one taking video of the entire proceeding. Half a dozen of the onlookers had their phones up in the air, recording everything.

How often did the masses get such entertainment?

Dancer was finally being recognized for their genius. Though they had been using public places to display their art, they now realized that they needed to go much more public.

Would it be possible to take over a stage at one of the local music festivals? Maybe arrange a body to drop down during the world-famous international film festival? Oh, the possibilities were endless!

So were the risks. It would be much more difficult to arrange something during one of those. Too many people around.

Still, Dancer had to do something. They reveled in the adoring crowd of bystanders. The fear they felt was palpable, particularly when the people around them realized that there had been a body *inside* the car.

Couldn't they smell the burning flesh? Or were their senses so dulled with fake news, fake food, and fake beer, that they couldn't recognize true artistry?

Although Dancer was sad to let one of their prized possessions go. They recognized it as a necessary loss, however. Breaking eggs, making omelets, like that.

The media had gotten their full share of the view as well. Dancer couldn't wait to get back home to their recordings. It would be a double treat, first here, to watch everything in person, then to see it again from different angles in the privacy of their home.

And that tall woman who'd been one of the closest to the car. Dancer had almost mistaken her for Billy Evans. Had she just been an innocent bystander? Or was she more involved? When she'd first seen the car, she'd immediately gone into the police station. Had she recognized it? Who was she, exactly?

Excitement stirred in Dancer's belly as the cameras swept across the crowd. They knew the police would also pore over the footage. Arsonists were frequently caught at the scene of their crime.

This wasn't a crime, however. This was an exorcism. A ritual of burning flesh to purify Dancer's soul, to ready them for the next step.

While the theme of the first three installations could have been chrysalis, Dancer found that predictable.

No, those first three scenes represented Dancer's true journey.

First, they'd been bound by the heaping disdain of society, of Dancer's family and "friends", including Billy and his ilk. Then there was the time when Dancer went under the knife and removed that irksome piece of flesh between their legs as they did a full, honest assessment of who they were, exactly, the piercing realizations of their normality amongst the deviants.

The third had represented Dancer finally flying free of all labels. They had transcended gender, as well as gross human needs.

Their needs had become eternal, like the gods they had overtaken.

Of course, Dancer was still a trickster, and a joker, as Warren had amply demonstrated.

Now, Dancer had been purified by the flame. Could let go of the past.

There would be one last magnificent kill before they would leave their cocoon and fly free. Land somewhere else and begin the infection of fear all over again.

CHAPTER 22

"You look like hell," Phoenix commented as they walked across the parking lot of the shared office space. Halley had suggested meeting there before heading out for their "stakeout." Phoenix was in their usual regalia that morning, wearing a long-sleeved navy blue evening gown that shimmered as they walked, along with silver pumps and a silver-furred wrap over their shoulders. The oversized silver purse they carried matched the shoes.

Halley shivered looking at them, though she wore a heavy leather jacket that covered her butt, along with fleece-lined leggings and heavy winter boots.

Was Phoenix wearing extra layers under that dress? Was that what kept them warm through the biting cold? The morning was gray and foggy, not rainy but misty, the kind that always damped Halley's mood. She preferred either sunny or a good downpour, not this shit that couldn't seem to make up its mind. Leaves swirled around her boots, though she couldn't hear them over the ringing that still echoed in her head.

"Being in an explosion will do that to you," Halley said

slowly. Everything seemed to be coming slowly that morning. Her words. Her steps. Even her thoughts.

"You were there?" Phoenix exclaimed.

Halley nodded, then realized that she really shouldn't be moving her head much at all. "I was," she said. "I was the one who identified the car."

"Warren's car?" Phoenix said.

"Yes," Halley said, barely remembering not to nod this time. "And there was a body inside. Theodore Lewis. His wife had filled out a missing person's report a few weeks before. Had already supplied dental records." The ME must have been working overtime in order for the body to have been identified so quickly.

Phoenix grew strangely still at the news. "You're kidding me," they said after a few moments.

Or maybe Halley's perception of time was all messed up. "Nope. Theodore 'Teddy' Lewis. Friend of yours?"

"He grew up just two houses down from me," Phoenix confessed.

Interesting. The press had already been expounding about the mansion he still lived in—his family home—out on Mercer Island.

So Phoenix really had come from money. Did they still own property out on the island with the other millionaires?

"Also, just a few houses away from Billy Evans," Phoenix added archly. "I had planned on staking out the Lewis' house for the next few days."

"Did you suspect that Teddy was actually Dancer in Darkness?" Halley asked, the pieces slowly coming together through the molasses that seemed to take up most of her brain that morning.

"I did," Phoenix said. They sighed. "Ted had a difficult childhood. His parents had a nasty divorce midway through sophomore year. Made the news, even. Everyone was gossiping about his mom's various lovers. She'd never been shy about her sexuality, exposing herself, walking around half naked, even in front of us. It was embarrassing as a kid, and I know it embarrassed the hell out of Ted. Plus, he was being abused by his father, but there wasn't anything I could do about it. I was just a kid, and we didn't have the knowledge or the resources that kids have these days."

Halley swallowed past a dry throat. She understood the guilt. She hadn't really known about her own mother's alcoholism, hadn't really recognized it, until after she'd started studying criminal justice. "So in classic terms, Ted had the right background for becoming a serial killer. Abusive father, inappropriately sexual mother."

Phoenix pressed their lips together in a firm line, as if they didn't want to continue. Finally, they added, "And Ted was a dancer. His mom made him take formal ballroom dancing. I know he got teased for it. Hell, I teased him about it." Phoenix's voice turned into a low growl. "That was, until I realized how furious Ted's dad was about it. Ted missed a week of school around that time. Flu, he claimed. But he'd moved so stiffly afterward. Never teased him about it again."

"Wow," Halley said. She'd never had to deal with that.

"Things got better for him," Phoenix said. "Ted showed up for Homecoming dance and was really able to move, was unafraid to dance with all the girls. Made a lot of guys jealous." They gave a bitter laugh. "He had no problems getting dates from then on. I heard far too many details about his various conquests." They added, "In addition, he grew cruel as he grew older. Much more so than the other people from the neighborhood. He was one of the first I cut out of my life."

"But Ted can't be the killer, not if it was his body in the car," Halley said.

"I know," Phoenix said, frustrated. "I still think there's

some connection there. Ted did have a brother, Kenny, but he left Seattle ages ago."

"Could it be Mr. Lewis? His father?" Halley suggested.

"He has neither the brains nor the imagination of Dancer in Darkness," Phoenix said, dismissing the man. "Though he did have that level of cruelty and perversion."

The image of Warren's desecrated body flashed before Halley's eyes. She felt her face blanch. Still, she continued on. Grit was something she already had in abundance before joining law enforcement. They'd just deepened the supply that had been there. "Was Ted married?"

Phoenix snorted. "Mail-order bride. Caralita Venzuago came from Mexico and arrived in the country only two weeks before the marriage. It was quite the scandal."

"How long ago was that?"

"Less than a year ago," Phoenix said. They sighed. "And Dancer has been at this for at least eighteen months. So it isn't her, either."

"So I'm guessing that we aren't doing a stakeout today then?" Halley said.

Phoenix cocked their head to one side. "We could always go and interview the recently widowed Mrs. Lewis."

"Would she talk with us?" Halley said. "I mean, she's probably inundated with reporters at this point."

"Let me make some calls," Phoenix said. "You, go inside the office and rest," they added sternly. "You look as if the least little wind is going to knock you on your ass."

Halley wanted to say something about how it was a good looking ass, but she couldn't find the words. God, she was tired. She nodded and headed back inside the shared office space, wondering if she could rent the smaller conference room on the first floor for the day and then nap on the floor under the table.

IT was midafternoon before Phoenix was able to arrange an interview with Mrs. Lewis. Halley took the time to sleep in her own bed for a few hours, feeling better after that. And more coffee.

The day had stayed cold and misty. It didn't start raining properly until they were on I-90, crossing over to Mercer Island.

Phoenix gave Halley directions by rote, as they had their head craned to the side, looking out. "Haven't been back in a while," they said. "Just seeing what's changed."

Halley nodded. She felt the same way every time she went back to Spokane. It wasn't building up as rapidly as Capitol Hill in Seattle, but it still was nothing like the town that she'd grown up in.

Phoenix directed Halley into one of the more exclusive neighborhoods on the island. Halley was surprised there wasn't a gate on the main road, barring access. The houses here were huge. More than one was set off from the street by a perfect yard that was big enough to have its own mini-golf course. None of them were decorated for Christmas yet. She imagined the show here would be tasteful, though.

They ended up on a street that was located above the houses. On the one side of the street, the houses were on the slope, below the road, looking out directly on Lake Washington. The other side of the road also had huge houses, built up, but without direct lake access. The lake was a metal gray, darkly reflecting the clouds above. Groves of lush pines were interrupted by stands of bare, naked trees, their fall splendor long since fallen. The grass here was still brilliant green, tended with loving care by its owners and their servants.

It surprised Halley that there weren't any news vans set

up on the road. Maybe Mrs. Lewis was already old news. Or she'd held her press conference already, or had agreed to talk with the press come Monday, as it was the weekend and no one wanted a big case to break until Monday.

"Why did Mrs. Lewis agree to meet up?" Halley said as they got out of the car. She pulled her leather coat around her tighter as the wind from the lake rushed out to greet them.

"I explained that I was an old friend of Theodore's," Phoenix said. "And was coming to express my condolences. She specifically asked no food be brought, though."

"I'm just your butch girlfriend?" Halley asked with a grin.

"Only in your dreams," Phoenix replied archly. "Particularly in that coat."

"What's wrong with this coat?" Halley said. She liked this coat.

"Oh I'm sure it was considered stylish back when you bought it, say, in 1999," Phoenix said.

Halley snorted. "This coat is only three years old," she pointed out.

"Then maybe it's the individual who could use some updating," Phoenix said as they reached the door.

Before Halley could reply, a tiny woman answered the door. Halley hated herself for assuming it was the help before she introduced herself as Caralita Lewis.

She had long black hair and darker skin that spoke of her Hispanic background. However, Halley heard no accent in the woman's voice. Had it been trained out of her?

Heavy eyeliner outlined Caralita's eyes, making her expression seem even darker. She had a small nose but a wide, generous mouth. She looked like a doll, with her perfect skin and perfect makeup. She wore a loose long-sleeved red blouse with a splotchy pattern of white—hibiscus flowers crowding in on one another. Her black slacks covered short, squat legs. All her height was in her torso. Around her neck was a black velvet choker, with a red flower in the center of it, made of garnets.

Caralita barely glanced at the pair of them before saying, "Come in."

That surprised Halley—generally people had more of a reaction to Phoenix. But Caralita Lewis hadn't reacted in the slightest.

Strange.

Mrs. Lewis led them through a dark entranceway to the left, into the living room. Floor to ceiling windows filled the far walls and showed off the backyard. Flower gardens ran along the edges of what appeared to be a new wooden privacy fence, at least six to eight feet tall running the length of the yard. Odd lumps covered in grass were scattered across what should have been a completely flat yard. Were they deliberate? A sort of natural raised flower bed? Lake Washington lay like a gray smudge past the green grass. The yard ended abruptly, a climbable set of rocks leading down to the shore. It appeared that the Lewises' didn't have a private boat access.

An ugly olive-green leather sofa took up one side of the room, faced by a pair of brown leather chairs that looked even more uncomfortable. To the right stood a large fireplace, the bricks recently painted white. A huge flat-screen TV lorded over the mantel.

Mrs. Lewis took one of the smaller chairs. Phoenix flowed in beside her, which left Halley the couch. It turned out to be just as uncomfortable as the chairs had looked, the seats too deep for even someone of Halley's size to sit back without strain.

"We're so sorry for your loss, my dear," Phoenix said, their deep voice full of soothing strains.

"Thank you," Mrs. Lewis said. She looked down at her hands, folded in her lap. "We weren't always close. But I still loved him."

Were they not close because she'd married for money? Had it been some sort of arranged marriage? Or was it because, as Phoenix had said, Ted had grown cruel as he'd aged?

"When was the last time you saw Ted?" Halley asked when Mrs. Lewis didn't go on.

"Friday, two weeks ago, just before I left to go visit my sister," Mrs. Lewis said. "I made him breakfast." She smiled at that, as if it had been something special. Then her smile fell. "He didn't want me to go. He was on his way out of town, and he still didn't want me to go."

She swallowed hard. Halley glanced at her throat, at the pretty choker she wore. Something seemed slightly off, there.

"Then the Uber came and I left. Maybe if we hadn't fought he'd still be here," Mrs. Lewis said, her voice breaking.

"No, ma'am, it wasn't your fault," Halley assured her. Though she'd never done a notification of death, she'd trained for it. "The killer came after him."

"Maybe he would have been more careful if we hadn't argued," Mrs. Lewis said, looking up from her lap and directly into Halley's eyes for the first time. She seemed so petite and small, like a fading flower. Halley had the irrational urge to protect this woman. Her demureness seemed to flow from her naturally, giving her an almost Victorian Lady air.

"No. It wasn't your fault," Halley repeated to her firmly.

"Not in the least," Phoenix added, their soothing tones blanketing the room with comfort.

Mrs. Lewis blinked a few moments, as if considering whether to believe them or not, then she looked down at her hands again.

"He never called after that. Never texted. I don't know where he went. I got worried by Monday when I still hadn't heard from him."

Halley heard something false in Mrs. Lewis' account. She couldn't say what. Just her ear, long trained in detecting falsehoods, was catching on something.

Mrs. Lewis was lying, but about what?

Had she actually been worried after she'd stopped hearing from her husband? Or had she gotten angry instead that he'd disappeared? Or possibly, if Phoenix was right and Mr. Lewis had grown cruel, had she been relieved?

"I filled out a missing person's report on Monday," she said. "Because I was so worried."

Again, Halley didn't believe the details. She glanced down at Mrs. Lewis' hands. One rubbed against the other, along the edge of her right forefinger.

Was that a bruise?

Halley suddenly felt sickened. She knew the cycle of abuse that went on, all too well. Fathers abused sons, who grew up to be abusers. Was Mrs. Lewis so conflicted because she was actually relieved that the bastard was gone?

"Was there anyone who was angry with Mr. Lewis?" Halley asked. She was aware that they weren't necessarily showing the support that Phoenix had said they were there to give. Hopefully Mrs. Lewis was too grief-stricken to really notice.

Mrs. Lewis looked up again, giving Halley a brittle smile. "I know I'm supposed to say that no, everyone loved Teddy. But they didn't. He was mean sometimes. Cruel. He had more enemies than friends."

That rang true. Halley glanced at Phoenix, who merely nodded.

"I tried to be a good wife," Mrs. Lewis said. She turned

to speak to Phoenix. "I tried to always support him, and to not respond when people said nasty things about him."

Halley found that she wasn't really listening anymore, arrested by Mrs. Lewis' profile.

That choker on Mrs. Lewis' neck was a good distraction. It drew the eye away from what was there.

"I'm sure you did, dear," Phoenix said. They didn't reach out to pat Mrs. Lewis' hand, though Halley thought they might. "I'm sure you did everything you could for him."

The pair of them left shortly after that. Halley had thought to ask about seeing Mr. Lewis' study, but Phoenix rushed them out of there, not wanting to take up the "poor dear's" time.

It wasn't until they were at the car that Phoenix said anything. "Did you see what I saw?" they asked, their voice a deep growl.

Halley nodded. "That wasn't a woman."

CHAPTER 23

PHOENIX DIRECTED Halley to a nearby coffeeshop, part of the main drag running through the island. "Who do you think that was? Exactly?" Halley asked after they'd sat down in an isolated corner. They could barely hear themselves over the loud shrieks of the three young children playing in the far corner, their harried mothers focused on each other, trying desperately to get a break. The concrete floor didn't help, and all the tables were metal. Despite the cheery light green paint covering the walls and the exotic flowers in test tubes hanging on them, it still seemed dim and chaotic.

"Someone who is transitioning," Phoenix said. "While their jaw line was still masculine, they had no trace of stubble. They've probably already had laser surgery to remove all their facial hair. Their makeup blending techniques were superb, and I couldn't detect a flaw in the coverage. They still need to get their Adam's apple broken, though the choker was a good distraction."

"Was that Dancer?" Halley had to ask.

Phoenix sighed. "Maybe?" they said. "It may also have been Caralita Lewis. I've never met the woman. Maybe Ted's bride was always transitioning."

"Can you find pictures from the wedding?" Halley asked. "Ask your friends?" That would be one way of making certain that the person they'd met that afternoon was actually Mrs. Lewis.

"I can try," Phoenix said. "However, that wouldn't be enough, would it? To get the police involved?"

"On the one hand, suspicion is always going to fall on the wife," Halley said. "On the other hand, it's a known serial killer, who was supposedly active before the wife even arrived in the country. Chances are, she's already been cleared."

"We need more evidence," Phoenix said. "And quickly."

"Do you think that Dancer has already found their next victim?" Halley asked, confused. Yes, Dancer had killed three people in as many weeks. That didn't mean that they would stay on that trajectory. There was a chance that they'd go back to their former pattern. Or they could continue to escalate.

"I'd wondered if you'd seen them," Phoenix said. "Sitting on the table next to the front door. Brochures from moving companies."

"Crap," Halley said. "If that is Dancer, they're going to move away. Start their games up somewhere else. Continue the cycle of violence."

"Exactly," Phoenix said, their voice more dry and bitter than Halley had ever heard it before. "We need to go back. Do that stakeout. See if we can find anything, anything at all, that we could bring to the police."

"All right," Halley said. She could do that. Watch from a distance.

Phoenix put their large silver handbag on the table, rummaged around in it for a few moments, before pulling out their small, delicate looking wallet and phone. "Here," they said, shoving the bag across the table. "You'll need this."

The bag was heavy. Too heavy. What the hell was Phoenix carrying?

"You go back to the house," Phoenix directed. "I have some phone calls to make. Let's see what dirt I can dig up on Mrs. Lewis. Or Caralita, for that matter."

They arranged to meet for dinner. Phoenix would bring carry-out to Halley, relieve her from the stakeout.

Halley used the restroom at the coffee shop before returning to her car.

In addition to pepper spray, Halley found what she'd been afraid of: a small Colt Mustang .380. It almost looked like a toy it was so tiny, with a blue steel and cute silver grips, but the tritium sights meant Phoenix wasn't messing around. It was heavier than it looked. After checking the ammunition —safety slugs, of course—as well as the safety, Halley slipped it into a jacket pocket before she washed her hands at the sink.

God, she looked like shit. Her brown hair was frazzled, the humidity playing havoc with it, despite how she'd conditioned it that morning. Her skin was pale and the dark circles under her eyes made them almost look bruised. The ringing noise in her ears had subsided to the point that she could mostly ignore it, but it still bothered her.

She made herself smile, that casual, friendly look that she could fake so well, that most people bought, thinking that Halley didn't have a concern in all the world.

Yup. Even that looked strained today.

Fuck 'em. She had a job to do. Possibly a serial killer to stop.

Phoenix would have to be the glamorous looking one today.

CHAPTER 24

THE AFTERNOON HAD ALREADY GROWN dark by the time Halley returned to watch the Lewis' house. Streetlights struggled to light their way through the fog that had gathered. The cold seemed to settle into Halley's bones, as she didn't want to start the car and draw attention to herself.

Was Mrs. Lewis actually Dancer in Darkness? Or had Mrs. Lewis always been in transition? They did make an excellent woman, being of smaller statue. However, despite supposedly coming from Mexico, the lack of an accent had set Halley's radar off. And maybe Halley had been around Phoenix too long, spent too much time with Roxy as well as watching other drag queens perform on YouTube. There had been something false about Mrs. Lewis from the start.

Halley wasn't back at her post for too long before she saw Mrs. Lewis drive away in her little Fiat convertible. She bet that was another way that Mr. Lewis had controlled his wife —not giving her a bigger car, more able to handle bad weather.

After debating for a few moments, Halley got out of the car and stomped her feet, trying to wake herself back up. The cold dove into her lungs with every breath. This was the sort of evening for walking to the local little wine bar just down the street from her condo that had a huge fake fireplace in the corner, then ordering hot chocolate laced with peppermint schnapps or even brandy.

Halley had no idea how long before Mrs. Lewis would return. She knew she should just hop back into her car, maybe run it for a while to get it warmed back up.

She absolutely did *not* want to break into the house. That was a surefire way to not only get herself arrested, but to get any evidence she found thrown out of court.

However, Halley did want to take a closer look at the property. Those odd mounds in the backyard bothered her. They felt so out of place with the pristine look of the rest of the neighborhood and their yards.

She took two deep breaths, then scurried forward, determined to get to the yard and back in under two minutes. As she rapidly approached the front door, she slowed.

The front door was open. She could see a sliver of light from inside slicing across the dark flagstones.

It wasn't technically breaking and entering if the door was already open. Halley could always say that she heard something.

Besides, she really wanted to get a look at the brochures from the moving companies, see if, as a last resort, they could follow Mrs. Lewis to the next city.

Halley used her gloved hand to push the door open. She took a deep breath, feeling the heat from the house wrap warm arms around her. God, it felt so good.

Before Halley could take another step inside, she heard a muffled yell.

Was that an actual cry for help? She cautiously stepped into the hallway.

Yes. That was someone pleading, screaming, crying.

Halley knew she should call Dick, Phoenix, someone, anyone. Mrs. Lewis could be back at any minute. But the screams downstairs sounded desperate.

Earlier that afternoon, Mrs. Lewis had brought them around through the left of the front hallway. This time, Halley went to the right, stepping into an expansive, modern kitchen that looked about as lived in as the Strauss'. A door on the left wall opened up to a staircase leading down to the basement.

All the lights were on both upstairs as well as downstairs. After glancing around for a moment, Halley cautiously made her way down the stairs.

The concrete floor felt cold underneath her boots. The first piece of equipment she saw was a large spanking stand made out of black padded leather and wood, used to tie a submissive to, to make it easier to beat them.

Dried blood stained the sides.

Beyond that, whips, floggers, canes, and paddles were carefully lined up on a table pushed up against a side wall. Along with a couple of weighted saps that looked as though they were made out of leather and possibly professional grade.

A tall St. Andrew's cross stood in the corner. A large man, naked to the waist, was tied to it. Red welts raised in long stripes crisscrossed his back. He was an older man based on the gray in his hair. His crying had quieted. Then he moaned, loud enough to wake the dead.

Halley reached for her phone to call for backup. She heard a noise behind her. Before she could turn around, something struck the back of her head and darkness overwhelmed her senses.

CHAPTER 25

Halley woke to a blistering headache. Black dots still swam before her eyes. Her arms were stretched out in front of her. Something supported her torso. She was standing, with her legs spread. Her leather jacket was conspicuously missing, as well as her shirt and exercise bra. The cold of the basement floor was already making its presence known through her stocking feet.

She tried to move, but found herself locked to the spanking stand she'd walked past earlier. Each ankle was locked in a metal cuff to one of the back legs of the stand. Then she was strapped over the stand, wrists cuffed to the front of it.

Halley jerked back, hoping that there was some give in the cuffs. Metal rattled.

No give. She was firmly attached. The room spun and her head pounded harder. She breathed through her nose so she didn't vomit.

The tall man was still bound to the St. Andrew's cross. He appeared to have recovered some, and was looking over his shoulder, glaring at the scene behind him.

"There's my lovely Halley girl!" came a voice from

Halley's side. "My, don't you look a treat all trussed up that way?"

Halley couldn't help but pull back again, the rattling of the metal links making her shudder.

It was a sound that was likely to give her nightmares from now on.

If she survived.

"You're perfectly safe here," said the voice, sliding gentle fingers up along her spine, making her shiver and goosebumps break out across her shoulders.

Finally, Halley saw the individual. She recognized Caralita Lewis from the bone structure, though the person in front of her was no longer wearing makeup. Or any clothes, for that matter.

Halley remembered the pictures she'd seen of Theodore, before he'd been killed. This person bore a striking resemblance to him.

Was this the Kenny that Phoenix had mentioned? The little brother who had supposedly moved away so long ago?

Their head was shaven smooth, and their arms and shoulders were muscular, sculpted. While they didn't have any breast implants, no penis remained, no testicles, either. They had a soft shape to their hips, however, curves that looked more womanly.

Halley wasn't about to heap abuse on Kenny, call them a Ken doll, though that was the unfortunate reference that came immediately to her mind.

No, it was much better for Halley to think of the person in front of her as Dancer, not as Kenny.

"I've always craved an audience," Dancer admitted as they stroked Halley's hair back from her face.

Her skin flushed both hot and cold from disgust of someone, anyone, touching her while she was so vulnerable.

If only she could vomit on cue. That might put Dancer off, though it might also get her whipped.

"You see, I was taught how important being watched was at an early age. Daddy Dearest would use me in front of Teddy, so that my big brother would learn the proper way to do it."

Halley shuddered. She didn't want to know this, how either of the Lewis boys had been brought up. It made sense how cruel Ted had grown, though, as a coping mechanism for handling the abuse.

"You disgust me," the man on the cross said. "You were always too soft. And now, look at you. You've turned yourself into a girl," he sneered.

"But isn't that what you wanted me to be?" Dancer asked. "That was how you used me."

"I had to discipline you in the only way you seemed to respond to," the man said.

It finally dawned on Halley that the man hanging from the cross was Richard Lewis, the father of both Kenny and Teddy.

"You abused your own son," Halley said. "Sons."

"Bah. They only now call it child abuse. When I was growing up, that sort of thing was just expected. You young people are all soft."

Halley blinked, astonished. Was the old man really that dumb? Or was he deliberately antagonizing Dancer, hoping that maybe his death would be quick?

Dancer didn't grow angry, though. They merely smiled. "You started me toward enlightenment," they said. "Encouraged me to transcend gender. And for that, I thank you. But you never recognized my brilliance. You will, tonight."

Before Richard Lewis could say anything else, Dancer

picked up one of the paddles lying on the table next to the cross and stuck the man's ass with all their might.

The howl Richard Lewis released chilled Halley to the bone. It made her realize just how alone they were here. No close neighbors, in the basement of a large mansion.

No one could hear them, or would even expect them to be there. Phoenix would find Halley's SUV abandoned, but wouldn't dare come into the house.

Dancer continued their beating, striking Mr. Lewis again on the ass, on the thighs and ribs, concentrating all their efforts on the main part of the torso.

"Just getting him softened up!" Dancer explained as they put the paddle away. They brushed Halley's hair back from her eyes again. "Don't worry. You're next."

Halley jerked back again, trying to escape. The cuffs cut into her bare skin. They were attached to the stand with metal carabiners, the clip kind, not the ones that twisted to lock.

Maybe if she could get enough room, she could twist her hand far enough to undo one…

Dancer put their nose up in the air and sniffed deeply. "Ah, there. That lovely scent of fear. I live on it, you know. The fear in the voice of body after they give up sense. The terror of a male as their fondest organ is pierced. The inexorable anguish as the moment of death approaches."

"How do you plan on displaying the body?" Halley asked. As much as she might not care for the old man, she didn't like watching him being beaten.

"See? Here's someone who can appreciate my art." Dancer came over and leaned one sweaty hip next to Halley's face. "The first art installation was a cocoon," Dancer said.

Halley hadn't seen any of the crime scene photos, but she nodded as if it all made sense.

As she'd told Dick earlier, police procedure one-oh-one:

Appear to empathize with the perpetrator, make them feel as if you're actually on their side.

"Then comes the piercing realization of self, the becoming of self," Dancer said, indicating their smooth body.

Halley wondered what she might have seen from the photos—had it been a grotesque collection of needles sticking out of every part of the body?

But she didn't let herself dwell on that. Instead, she thought about what she'd read about the third installation, how the body had been deliberately placed, hung above the stage.

"Then, the third installation, that was you dancing, flying free," Halley guessed.

"Give the girl a gold star!" Dancer said. "Did you really see that journey in my art?" they asked, their eyes wide and curious as a child's.

"I did," Halley lied. Had she just heard a soft thump behind her? Was there someone else in the house?

She had to keep talking. Keep Dancer's attention focused on her. On the off chance that maybe Phoenix had found her empty car and called the police. "But what was Warren?"

"Warren meant nothing. Beyond a fool," Dancer said dismissively. "As you might label it, a crime of opportunity."

"And Ted?" Halley asked. She had to know.

Dancer gave a cruel smile. "You know he kept me here, right? Tried to control me. Poured money into keeping my story out of the system, out of the public eye. Made up that tale of me moving away, even paid off a doctor to fake records of my being treated so very far away."

"But what happened?" Halley said. Something had to have set Dancer off, had to have made them escalate.

"Billy did! When he arrived in town, it was time to bring all the boys back home." Dancer paused, then walked back over to where Halley was confined. "You know, the pair of you look remarkably similar," Dancer said. They pulled Halley's head back abruptly, the pain of it making her wince. Dancer turned her head to the right and left, considering. "I wonder if you're actually related. You should ask your own Mommy Dearest."

"I wouldn't ask that bitch for a glass of water if I were on fire," Halley growled. Part of the emotion she poured forth was just building empathy. Part of it, though, was honest enough. While she wouldn't want her mother to change places with Richard Lewis—no one deserved to be beaten that way, not even her mother—she wouldn't mind possibly giving her a scare bad enough to frighten her to get sober.

"I understand," Dancer said. "We're really not that far apart, are we?"

Halley made herself smile up at the monster who still tugged at her hair, her scalp smarting, her eyes watering. At least the pain there was overriding the harsh pounding from the back of her head.

"Both of us playing the part that the world has handed us. You, making do after leaving the police force," Dancer continued. "Me, practicing and perfecting my art, appearing as Caralita even after she was gone. Teddy was devastated. I think he understood that the milk I gave him that morning for breakfast was poisonous. He was ready to go."

"How did Caralita die?" Halley asked. Yes, that was definitely a sound behind her. There was someone else downstairs.

"Now, we all have our trade secrets, don't we?" Dancer said. "It was a shame that I couldn't display that body. But really, she was just practice. Like the others."

Halley forced herself to keep smiling as she realized the implications.

The backyard. Those odd mounds. How many bodies were buried back there?

"Every artist must practice their art, right?" Dancer said, finally releasing Halley's head.

Black spots again swam before her eyes. She had some sort of concussion, she was certain. That wasn't going to save her, though.

She pulled more quietly on the cuffs. Could she get free? Before it was "her turn"?

"And now? What's your latest art installation going to be?" Halley asked, trying to get Dancer to talk more, before they beat Richard Lewis to death in front of her.

Dancer peered at Halley, looking quizzical. "You're not afraid. Why not? You should be very afraid. You're tied up. You're going to be next." Dancer paused, their eyes narrowing. "You are talking too much. Why?"

"I talk when I get nervous," Halley explained easily.

Dancer considered that for a moment. "I'm not sure I believe you. Billy doesn't. He gets still and quiet when he's upset or nervous."

Halley did her best to give a casual shrug, which was difficult given how she was stretched out. "Maybe we aren't related."

Dancer raised their head and sniffed, like a hound catching a scent. Then they raced to where Mr. Lewis was still hanging.

"Shoot me and you shoot him," Dancer proclaimed. They pressed the gun Halley had been carrying to Richard Lewis' temple, forcing him to turn his head to the side. They couldn't miss from that close.

"My dear Dancer, why would I shoot an artist such as yourself?" came the cultured tones of Phoenix. "You know, you have many admirers in the community," they continued, coming further into the room.

Dancer looked perplexed. "I would have thought it was Billy coming in here, not you, Marc. Billy also knew of the loose window at the back of the basement."

Phoenix snorted. "Why do we care about him?" they asked.

Halley could finally see Phoenix. They were still wearing their long navy blue evening gown, though they'd added a scarf around their neck so they were no longer showing any skin. Their dark hair glistened with raindrops. It must have grown quite wet outside. They must be wearing extra layers, as Halley could swear that their torso looked bulked up.

They had a gun in their hands. It matched the one in Dancer's.

Of course, Phoenix would have guns that matched. No wonder the rough handle was dark blue, not black. It also matched their outfit.

"The boys needed to talk," Dancer said. "Daddy dearest and Billy. About his own daddy. How he died."

"Mr. Evans?" Phoenix said. "What about Mr. Evans? Didn't he just kill himself?"

Though Halley couldn't say for certain, she felt that Phoenix had just been thrown a curveball.

Mr. Lewis gave a crackling laugh. "No, he didn't. I was there."

The sound of the gunshot rang through the basement, loud enough to hurt Halley's ears.

Why had Dancer just shot their father? Was it because of what he'd just said? What was the mystery about Billy's father?

"Let go of the gun!" Phoenix said, their soothing voice suddenly ravaged.

Dancer ignored Phoenix. They swung the gun around and pointed it at Halley's head.

At least they finally looked like the monster they were, with blood spattered across their face, their eyes wild.

"Why?" Halley asked. She had no question other than that. "Why kill him like that?"

"So that you will suffer as I did," Dancer said. "Suffer for your art, Halley. Suffer for the man who might have killed your actual father."

Dancer shifted to a wider stance, still pointing the gun directly at Halley's head.

"Don't do it," Phoenix warned. "Please. I beg of you. Let this one live."

Was Phoenix going to rush Dancer? As far as Halley knew, Phoenix didn't have any hand-to-hand training. Rushing a shooter that way would be the surest way of getting themself killed.

"Daddy Dearest wasn't the only one in the room," Dancer said. "I was there too."

They suddenly swung the gun toward Phoenix. Their hands tightened.

"Don't!" Halley cried out.

Too late. Dancer got off one shot.

Halley's head rang with the sound of the shot. She couldn't hear anything. Were they shouting at each other?

Phoenix staggered back. Then they deliberately raised their gun and shot Dancer.

Dancer went down.

CHAPTER 26

HALLEY WAS STILL MOVING SLOWLY, her ears still ringing, two days after Dancer had given her a concussion. She had to squat to pick anything up—bending over and inverting her head was just all kinds of bad. Everything she ate had a metallic taste, as if gunpowder coated her tongue.

Despite that, she was back at the shared office space that morning. Well, late morning. Brunch time, really. Phoenix had insisted that they meet again.

Halley sat in the smaller conference room downstairs, where she'd met Phoenix for the first time just one week before.

Had it only been a week? Halley felt so much older that morning. Or maybe that was still the concussion. She sipped carefully at her coffee, then grimaced at the taste. Damn it! She was not going to have coffee ruined for her. She added a dollop of cream to the cup, polluting it, just to coat her mouth.

Phoenix was exactly on time, something that Halley had come to appreciate. They wore the dark purple gown that Halley had seen them in the first time, though instead of a white fur stole they actually had a full jacket on, made out of a shimmering silver fur.

"Hello, my dear," Phoenix said as they came into the shared office space. "No, sit," they instructed as Halley started to rise. They stared at Halley's face for a moment, speculating. Then they bustled into the room. "Don't worry about it, I can fix it myself," they instructed, walking behind Halley to the sideboard and snagging some green tea.

"How are you?" Halley asked as Phoenix prepared their tea.

"Bruised. And that gown I was wearing? Ruined! Just ruined." Phoenix gave a dramatic sigh. "The things I'll do to help my fellow person."

Halley made the mistake of shaking her head. She stopped just before the room started spinning.

"More to the point, how are you doing?" Phoenix said, walking back to their side of the table and sitting across from Halley.

"Still sore," Halley admitted. "But recovering. And it was a good thing you were wearing body armor," she pointed out. She hadn't been imagining it—Phoenix had appeared more bulky than usual when they'd showed up in the Lewis' basement.

Phoenix nodded, momentarily sobered. "I'm just glad that I remembered that window, from when we'd been boys together."

"Had Dancer left it broken on purpose?" Halley asked.

Phoenix gave an exaggerated shrug. "Who knows? Kenny had grown quite insane. They obviously knew it was there. Did they keep the window broken so that they had an escape route if all else failed?"

Halley sighed but remembered not to shake her head. "Did you see the news about the backyard?"

"I did. What's the body count up to?"

"There were eight mounds," Halley said, remembering the yard clearly. "So I figure they've found at least eight bodies. Possibly more if Dancer doubled any of them up."

"Such a waste," Phoenix said, their beautiful voice catching. "So many lives wasted."

Halley didn't reply. She waited, instead, for Phoenix to get around to saying what they'd come to say. Or to ask.

"Are you getting your DNA tested? With Billy?" Phoenix finally asked. "Dancer thought you two might be related."

"Don't know," Halley admitted. "Seemed that his father had regular business in Spokane. We're meeting later this afternoon to talk about things."

"Ooooh," Phoenix said, obviously intrigued. "You'll have to tell me all about it."

Halley gave a non-committal shrug. She didn't know what would happen when she met with Billy. Wasn't sure what she wanted to happen.

"You do look very similar," Phoenix said after a moment. "I hadn't realized it until Dancer pointed it out."

"Mom always said I resembled her side of the family," Halley said, automatically defensive, though she'd always had the same doubts herself.

"Did you ask your dear mother about it?" Phoenix inquired.

Halley gave a derisive snort. "That would involve actually talking to her. Which I don't do. Not regularly." She had finally read the text from her sister, which had been full of further recriminations about how unfair Caroline's life was and how Halley had never been there for any of them, had never picked up after her own messes, and how she now needed to start paying for some of Mom's care.

Despite the fact that Mom wasn't in the care of anyone. Caroline was just looking for another handout.

"Well, you have other family you can turn to, if you need to," Phoenix declared.

Halley sighed. Family of choice was really all that was going to be left to her, particularly if Caroline went through with her threat to cut Halley off in retaliation.

Unless, of course, there was some sort of family with Billy…

"I also wanted to reassure you that I had no idea that little Kenny was Dancer," Phoenix added. "I'd thought they'd moved away. Everyone did. They hadn't come back for the wedding or anything."

"I know," Halley said. Dick had actually come out and told her that while collecting her statement. No one had suspected the little brother. He was supposedly committed to an institution, somewhere in Colorado.

Had there been a connection between Jennifer Strauss and her family and the Lewises? Probably that was where the initial connection had been made, the doctor willing to fake records.

That whole network of rich white boys doing favors for one another.

"So, what's next?" Phoenix asked Halley. "What other fabulous cases are we going to take on together?"

The feeling of incredulity struck Halley. Her heart started pounding hard, a ridiculous amount of adrenaline surging through her body. "I'm not sure I'm really in the market for a partner," she said.

"I know, I know. You're just afraid that I'm too glamorous for the life of a PI," Phoenix said, waving their hand in the air. "I have better makeup and disguise skills than anyone you know," they assured Halley. "Just you wait. Your next case will call for it."

Halley pressed her lips together so she didn't laugh out

loud. "I will certainly keep that in mind," she finally said with a mostly straight face.

"Until then, darling," Phoenix said, standing. "I shall relish the next time I hear from you. Toodaloo!"

They swept out of the room, the faint scent of jasmine and lavender remaining.

Did Phoenix really want to partner with Halley? She snorted. No. Halley's cases weren't all as glamorous, or as life threatening, as this one had been. None of them before had been. She was actually looking forward to the regular routine of just following people around again, stalking them online and elsewhere.

Halley contained her groan as she stood up, gathering up the cups and heading back to the kitchen to wash up. Luther was regaling someone else in the backroom with his latest research. She decided against joining them, instead heading out to meet her next client, Mrs. Farrow. She didn't feel up to the inevitable confrontation, however; she hated how much time she'd wasted investigating an innocent man.

When it had been Mrs. Farrow all along who'd been the guilty one.

It had taken a little more digging for Halley to find evidence of Mrs. Farrow's affair. Not proof, nothing that she could take to court. But enough to get the woman to back off investigating her own husband.

Firing Mrs. Farrow was going to feel so good. Halley was actually looking forward to it. She'd have to find more clients, but that was always the case. She wasn't living paycheck to paycheck. Too many people needed someone like her to dig up the muck on someone else.

But working with Phoenix hadn't paid any of her bills. She was going to have to remember that, the next time some "glamorous" case came up.

CHAPTER 27

CHRISTMAS WAS OVER, and the new year had set in darkly. Halley couldn't remember another time when the lack of lights bothered her so much. Still, she met with Billy late that afternoon, in a café close to the shared workspace.

She and Billy had agreed to get DNA tests done, to see if they were related. They both could see the resemblance, once it had been pointed out. They had the same hair. The same lanky height. Halley's eyes were blue while his were hazel, hers were spaced farther apart, but they shared a similar look.

The DNA tests had shown up that morning, and they were meeting to compare notes. Halley clutched her unopened envelope while waiting for her turn with the angry barista. Billy came in a short time later, though he foolishly got a bottle of water instead of the elixir of life.

Halley and Billy had only met twice before the holidays too coordinate things. He was still harried, working homicide in King County over the Christmas holidays.

"Shall we?" Billy said as he sat down. He slid his envelope across the table over to her.

In return, Halley gave hers to Billy.

How stupid for her adrenaline to kick in. Since the encounter with Dancer, though, she'd found herself on more of a hair trigger than before.

They both opened the envelope they were holding, pulling out the results simultaneously.

All Halley could see on the page she held was the single word.

Match.

They were related, with a little less than half of their chromosomes matching.

"Okay," Halley said, as she put the paper down on the tiny table. Billy did the same. She took a deep drink from her coffee. Billy drank from his water bottle. Silence consumed them.

Mom had had an affair. Three years after Caroline had been born. She'd always said that Halley had been an unexpected gift.

Had Dad ever realized that Halley wasn't his? He'd never given any indication of that. Then again, he hadn't ever been around that much, working all the time instead.

Mom sure as shit knew.

Could Halley ask her? She hadn't said anything when she'd traveled back to Spokane for Christmas, having skipped Thanksgiving, still having a spat with Caroline. They had kind of made up, at least for a little while. Spent a relatively peaceful Christmas all together, with her nephews and her mom.

"So what now?" Halley asked Billy finally.

He gave her a grin, one that she recognized. It was that easy-going smile that she faked frequently.

"I don't know. Sis," Billy said, deliberately teasing her.

"Big sis," Halley corrected, as according to their birth records, she'd been born nearly six months before him.

"Do you think it happened here in Seattle? Or back in Spokane?" Billy asked.

Halley shook her head. "Don't know. But I figure Spokane. Mom was never much of one to travel." Halley didn't even want to consider that it might have been rape.

Billy nodded. "Dad frequently had business out in Spokane. But I'm not sure what."

Halley had done some preliminary research on Mr. Evans, on his supposed suicide. As part of her report to the police, she'd told them that both Mr. Lewis and Kenny had claimed to have been in the office when Mr. Evans had killed himself. That part had never made it to the newspapers. Billy had interviewed Halley personally later, asking about it.

He'd hinted that his father had had some crooked dealings. It was why he'd been killed. Billy was adamant that it hadn't been a suicide.

"How do you want to investigate this?" Halley asked.

Billy gave her a sharp look.

"Oh, come on. You know you want to solve this puzzle as badly as I do," Halley said. "I doubt it will do any good to ask my mom. But I could go and see her doctor, to find out if there was anything about the pregnancy."

"I don't know," Billy said after a moment. "I'm not sure what that would turn up. If it would turn up anything useful."

Halley cocked her head to the side. There was a something more—a lot more—to this story than what Billy was telling her.

She thought for a moment as the pieces clicked together.

"You were out at Gonzaga, studying law, before your—our —father killed himself," Halley said. "You changed your major to criminal justice and joined law enforcement afterward. Was that so that you could continue the investigation into his death?"

Billy pressed his lips together instead of replying immediately.

That gave Halley all the answer she needed.

"You're still investigating his death, aren't you?" Halley said.

Billy's face had grown slightly pale. His eyes darted around the room, as if looking for an escape? Someone to help him? The right lie that Halley might possibly believe?

"It wasn't a suicide. Was it?" Halley stated flatly.

For a brief moment, she thought Billy might actually physically run away from her. Finally, the moment passed and Billy relaxed slightly.

"It wasn't," he said, shaking his head. "Not as far as I can tell. There are still too many questions. Too many inconsistencies. And now, with Mr. Lewis and Kenny..." He let the words hang.

"So where do we go from here?" Halley asked. When Billy hesitated again, she deliberately added, "Little brother?"

That got her at least a faint echo of that easy-going smile. "We do need to figure out if your mother or family were involved at all with mine, earlier," he said.

Halley gulped and nodded. "And you'll show me your case files, right?" she said.

Now it was Billy's turn to gulp and nod. "Yeah. I can."

They sat in silence for a few moment, sizing each other up.

Family. Or family of choice.

At least family that Halley was willing to associate with, for the time being.

She wasn't looking forward to driving back to Spokane. To talking with her mother, her mother's doctor, her sister. Maybe even Joel, her father's best friend. This was yet another case that she wasn't interested in taking.

And the pay wasn't going to be worth shit.

However, for once, she wasn't alone.

She raised her coffee cup to Billy, who raised up his own water bottle. They clinked the bottoms of their respective drinks together.

"To family."

"To family. Long may they live in Hell."

Leah Cutter writes page-turning fiction in exotic locations, such as a magical New Orleans, the ancient Orient, Hungary, the Oregon coast, rural Kentucky, Seattle, Minneapolis, and many others.

She writes literary, fantasy, mystery, science fiction, and horror fiction. Her short fiction has been published in magazines like *Alfred Hitchcock's Mystery Magazine* and *Talebones*, anthologies like Fiction River, and on the web. Her long fiction has been published both by New York publishers as well as small presses.

Find Leah's books on Knotted Road Press at (www.KnottedRoadPress.com)

Follow her blog at www.LeahCutter.com.

Reviews

It's true. Reviews help me sell more books. If you've enjoyed this story, please consider leaving a review of it on your favorite site.

Come someplace new…

Are you a traveler? Do you enjoy exploring strange new worlds, new cultures, new people?

Journey into the various lands envisioned by Leah Cutter.

Sign up for my newsletter and I'll start you on your travels with a free copy of my book, *The Island Sampler*.

I will never spam you or use your email for nefarious purposes. You can also unsubscribe at any time.

http://www.LeahCutter.com/newsletter/

ABOUT KNOTTED ROAD PRESS

Knotted Road Press fiction specializes in dynamic writing set in mysterious, exotic locations.

Knotted Road Press non-fiction publishes autobiographies, business books, cookbooks, and how-to books with unique voices.

Knotted Road Press creates DRM-free ebooks as well as high-quality print books for readers around the world.

With authors in a variety of genres including literary, poetry, mystery, fantasy, and science fiction, Knotted Road Press has something for everyone.

Knotted Road Press
www.KnottedRoadPress.com